DANCING IN THE DAYLIGHT

Ben Hafer

Library of Congress Cataloging-in-Publication Data

Names: Hafer, Ben, author
Title: Dancing in the Daylight: a novel / Ben Hafer
Identifiers: ISBN 979-8-9994438-1-6 (paperback)
ISBN 979-8-9994438-2-3 (hardcover)
ISBN 979-8-9994438-0-9 (ebook)
Subjects: GSAFD: Bildungsromans

Published in the United States

CHAPTER ONE

T he grating buzz of an old-school alarm clock shattered the tranquility of the early morning. Its red LED display cast a faint glow in the dim room, the blocky numbers frozen at 6:45 AM. Noah Harper's eyelids fluttered open, his gaze settling on the blurry red numbers. He groaned softly, the sound muffled by his pillow.

With a sigh, he reached out a hand from beneath the warm cocoon of his blankets. His fingers fumbled across the cluttered nightstand, brushing against the edges of dog-eared comic books and the cool plastic of a vintage cassette player. Finally, his hand found the off button, and with a decisive slap, the grating noise ceased, leaving the room in peaceful silence once more.

Noah lay there for a moment, staring up at the ceiling where faint cracks formed patterns only he could decipher. The soft morning light seeped through the gaps in his curtains, casting shadows over scattered VHS tapes littering the wooden floor. Titles like *The Breakfast Club*, *Ghostbusters*, and *Tron* peeked out from their worn cases, remnants of a time he felt more connected to than the present.

He reluctantly swung his legs over the side of the bed. As he stood, his eyes roamed over the posters plastered haphazardly on his walls. *Back to the Future* dominated the space above his desk, Marty McFly's confident grin looking down at him. To the right, *The Goonies* crew huddled together, exuding camaraderie and adventure. Next came *E.T.* pointing a glowing finger outward, as if urging Noah to reach for something beyond his grasp.

For Noah, those posters weren't just decorations— they were his escape routes, portals into worlds where everything felt bigger and more important than the monotony of everyday life. They reminded him that ordinary kids could do extraordinary things. He liked to imagine himself as part of those stories—standing beside Marty, shouting, "Great Scott!". Racing through a booby-trapped cavern with Mikey and Chuck. Or flying through the stars with E.T. on the handlebars of his bike. It was a comforting fantasy—one he often clung to on mornings like this when the weight of another school day pressed against his chest.

Yawning, Noah trudged to the bathroom, rubbing the sleep from his eyes. He flicked on the light, squinting momentarily at his reflection. His unruly curls stuck up in every direction, sleep leaving them even wilder than usual. He sighed, running his fingers through the dark mess in a futile attempt to tame it. His face was narrow, with freckles across his nose and cheeks. A pair of green eyes blinked back at him, framed by lashes still half-clumped together. Noah splashed cool water on his face, and flashed himself a lopsided grin, mimicking the movie heroes from his posters.

Satisfied enough with his efforts, he reached for his toothbrush and scrubbed at his teeth with the urgency of someone who'd rather be doing anything else. He added another splash of cold water to his still-groggy face, and ran damp fingers through his hair, pushing the stray strands back into something resembling order—just enough to look like he hadn't rolled straight out of bed, even if that was mostly true.

Before leaving the bathroom, he lingered by the mirror, tracing the faint outline of a crack near the corner of the glass. He'd stared at it a hundred times before, letting it become part of the background, but today, it caught his attention. It reminded him of how life had felt lately—small cracks forming under the surface, just out of sight. With a shake of his head, he turned off the light and headed back to his room.

Noah crossed the floor to his closet, pulling open the creaking door to reveal a jumble of clothes. Rummaging through the hangers, he bypassed the few newer items his mom bought him. Instead, he reached for his trusty denim jacket, its fabric worn soft by years of wear. The jacket was adorned with various pins and patches—a smiley face here, a peace sign there, and his favorite, a small, embroidered cassette tape on the left pocket.

Leaving his room he descended the narrow staircase, the familiar creak of the third step announcing his arrival. The aroma of freshly toasted bread mingled with the faint scent of coffee greeted him. In the tiny kitchen, his mom was already dressed in her uniform, her dark hair pulled back into a hurried ponytail. She was buttering a piece of toast with one hand while holding a travel mug in the other.

"Morning, sweetheart," his mom called without turning around, her voice cheerful.

"Morning," Noah mumbled, grabbing a glass from the cupboard.

"I made toast. Pop-Tarts are in the pantry if you're in the mood for dessert disguised as breakfast."

"Pop-Tarts, obviously," Noah said, crossing the kitchen to grab one. He unwrapped the foil and bit into it cold, leaning against the counter. "You've got an early shift today?"

She nodded, blowing on her coffee. "Yeah, Mrs. Thompson's out again, so it's all hands on deck at the pharmacy. You know how it is."

"You work too much," Noah said, his tone quieter now.

His mom waved him off with a laugh. "I could say the same about you and your late-night study sessions. Like mother, like son, right?"

"Yeah, but I don't get paid," Noah shot back with a grin.

His dad, seated at the table with his coffee and morning paper, looked over. "He's not wrong. You do work too much."

"And who exactly is going to cover for Mrs. Thompson if I don't?" she asked.

"Maybe Mrs. Thompson could just… not get sick," Noah offered.

His mom laughed lightly. "I'll bring that up next time she calls in."

His dad folded his paper and leaned into the conversation. "Your mom's a workhorse, no doubt about it. But she could definitely stand to slow down."

"Says the guy who comes home smelling like grease

and stress," she shot back with a raised eyebrow.

"Hey, that's called *strategy*," his dad said. "I'm just making sure we're ready for Disney this summer. Gotta save up for Space Mountain."

She smirked. "Space Mountain? Please. You're a Small World kind of guy."

"Bold of you to assume I wouldn't ride both," his dad shot back, deadpan.

Noah snorted, shaking his head. "You guys are too much."

His mom glanced at the microwave clock, her expression shifting. "Shoot, I'm gonna be late." She grabbed her keys from the hook by the door and leaned down to kiss Noah's forehead. "Be good, okay? Oh, we're having your favorite tonight—spaghetti and garlic bread."

"Fire," Noah said with a smirk, brushing crumbs off his jacket. "I'll bring my appetite."

"Love you, honey," she said with a smile, then headed out. The door clicked shut behind her, leaving the house quieter.

His dad stretched back in his chair, sipping his coffee. "So. Big day?"

Noah shrugged. "Just the usual I guess."

His dad leaned back in his chair. "Fair enough," he said, a thoughtful expression crossing his face. "High school's kind of like being stuck in a snow globe—looks nice from the outside, but inside, it's just a whole lotta spinning."

Noah raised an eyebrow. "That's... surprisingly accurate."

"Yeah, well." His dad leaned forward, elbows on the table. "When I was your age, I always figured I'd look back at high school as the best days of my life." He paused, shaking his head with a wry smile. "Here's the thing—nobody actually peaks in high school. If they do, it's just sad. You'll figure it out as you go. You've got time."

Noah gave a small smile. "I hope so. Just feels like a lot sometimes."

His father nodded. "It is a lot. But you're tougher than you think. Just take it one day at a time." He gave Noah a reassuring smile. "And remember, you don't have to figure it all out at once."

"Yeah, I know." Noah's voice was quiet.

"Good." His dad reached for his coffee mug and lifted it slightly in Noah's direction. "And if nothing else, there's always the little things to look forward to. Like Mom's awesome spaghetti."

He nodded, grinning. "Yeah, that's definitely something to look forward to."

"Atta boy." His dad returned the smile, his eyes holding a hint of pride. "Go on, now. You don't want to be late."

Noah slipped on his worn sneakers, the fabric frayed at the edges, and adjusted his backpack. As he pulled the front door open, the crisp morning breeze hit him, sharp and cool, carrying the faint scent of freshly cut grass. He paused for a moment and glanced back over his shoulder.

"Hey, Dad?"

His dad looked up. "Yeah?"

Noah hesitated, then smiled. "Thanks."

His dad's face softened. "Love you, bud."

Noah gave him a smile before stepping outside, letting the door click shut softly behind him.

He pulled up the hood of his jacket and slipped on his headphones. The opening synth beats of A-ha's "Take on Me" filled his ears, creating a kind of soundtrack to his morning.

Stepping onto the sidewalk, he began his familiar journey. The neighborhood was just waking up—cars idling in driveways, morning joggers passing by with earbuds in place, dogs barking at squirrels scampering up trees. Each house he passed was a mirror of the last: neatly trimmed lawns, mailboxes standing like sentinels at the end of each driveway.

He kept his gaze downward, the music in his ears providing a comforting barrier between him and the world—a bubble where he could retreat and let his imagination roam free. The upbeat rhythm of the song seemed to whisper promises of adventure, of something just beyond the horizon.

As he neared the school, the building's familiar outline came into view—a sprawling structure of brick and glass that seemed both imposing and mundane. Its towering facade was peppered with tall windows, each reflecting the early morning sun, and the flagpole out front fluttered in the light breeze. When he reached the end of the block, he veered off the main path, taking a shortcut through an empty lot.

Pushing aside a section of the chain-link fence where it hung loose and rusted, he stepped through, careful to avoid the twisted metal edges. The lot was overgrown, tall weeds brushing against his legs, and a few scattered soda cans and crumpled wrappers lay caught in the brambles. He kicked a rock that had nestled itself in the dirt, watching it bounce along the ground.

The earth was uneven here, and he stepped carefully, dodging patches of gravel and the occasional puddle from yesterday's rain. The smell of wet earth lingered as he made his way across, a few stubborn wildflowers still clinging to life among the weeds.

Ahead, he spotted the break in the fence on the other side of the lot, where someone had twisted it open enough for a person to slip through. He crouched slightly, slipping past the metal edge, and found himself back on the sidewalk, dusting off his hands.

Crossing the street, he nodded at Mr. Johnson, the crossing guard, who tipped his cap in return. The brief exchange made Noah feel like he was passing through scenes from a movie, with every person and place perfectly cast for his journey.

The schoolyard was alive with activity, a buzz of voices mingling with the occasional burst of laughter or shout. Clusters of students gathered in their usual spots: the athletes near the gym entrance, tossing a football back and forth, their laughter echoing across the yard; the drama kids under the big oak tree, animatedly discussing last night's rehearsal while striking exaggerated poses; and the band members on the front steps, some practicing riffs on their instruments while others tapped out rhythms on their knees.

Noah took a deep breath and slipped through the throng, sticking close to the outer edges of the crowd. He moved with purpose, his head down, eyes scanning for the best path forward without interruptions. He was adept at navigating the social labyrinth without drawing attention—a shadow blending seamlessly into the background. He passed by a group of students arguing over a math problem, and then sidestepped a pair of girls who were too busy laughing at something to notice him.

The bell tower loomed above, casting a long shadow across the courtyard. Noah glanced up briefly, catching sight of the clock—five minutes to the first bell. He picked up his pace, the hum of morning energy buzzing around him. It wasn't that he disliked people; it was more that he had perfected the art of avoiding unwanted interaction. He could nod at familiar faces, even exchange a quick greeting if necessary, but Noah preferred the comfort of staying out of sight, of slipping between the lines where nobody took much notice.

As he neared the side entrance, he spotted a few familiar faces—kids he shared classes with, but never really talked to. He gave a quick nod to a boy from his science class, who responded with a casual wave before returning to his conversation. Not that he would ever think to join in. Noah shifted his backpack on his shoulder, feeling the reassuring weight of his books, and stepped inside, the noise of the schoolyard fading as the door closed behind him.

The hallway was slightly quieter, but still full of movement. Lockers clanged open and shut, and a few teachers stood in their doorways chatting. Laughter echoed, and snippets of conversation floated through the air.

"Did you see the game last night?"

"I can't believe she said that!"

"Test in algebra today—I'm soooo not ready."

Noah made his way to his locker, spinning the combination lock with practiced ease. He opened the metal door to reveal a neatly organized space. A small mirror was taped inside, along with a faded photo of him and his dad at a baseball game years ago. He smiled at the memory, the sunlit day captured forever in that worn-out snapshot. He swapped out the books in his bag for the ones he'd need for the morning.

With everything in place, Noah closed the locker door with a clank, slipping his backpack onto his shoulder. He merged into the stream of students moving through the hallway as the first bell rang. Some walked in clusters, laughing loudly and bumping shoulders, while others moved with the same determination as Noah, focused on just getting where they needed to be.

He passed by a few kids crowded around a locker.

"Did you see what happened in gym yesterday?" one of them said.

"Yeah, Derek totally wiped out. Classic!" another voice responded, followed by a burst of laughter.

Noah kept his head down, avoiding eye contact but listening with half an ear to the snippets of conversation around him.

"I can't believe she said yes! Dude, the dance is gonna be amazing," a boy exclaimed to his friend, who slapped him on the back with a grin.

"Hey, did you finish the homework? I swear I can't figure out number five," someone else exclaimed.

Noah moved forward, his eyes on the floor ahead, weaving between students.

"Did you hear about Mr. Taylor? I heard he might be leaving," a girl told her friend.

"Seriously? No way. Who's gonna take over art class then?" the friend replied.

Noah tuned out the rest as he focused on his path, slipping through the gaps in the crowd. He was just another face in the hallway, blending into the background noise as the school came to life around him.

He reached the stairwell, and began to climb. The second floor was less crowded—students were starting to file into classrooms, and the bell would be ringing any minute. He took a left at the top of the stairs, heading down the corridor lined with posters advertising upcoming events: a school play, the next football game, a canned food drive. He paid them little mind as he continued down the hallway until he reached his history class.

Inside, the room was still filling up, students drifting in with varying degrees of enthusiasm. Some were animatedly discussing weekend plans, while others looked as though they'd rather be anywhere else. Noah slipped into his preferred seat by the window, placing his backpack on the floor beside him. He liked this spot—close enough to the front that he wouldn't be called out for hiding, but by the window where he could let his mind wander when things got dull.

He glanced outside, where a few students were still making their way in from the yard. The sun filtered through the trees, casting moving shadows across the grass. Noah took a deep breath, letting the quiet moment calm his nerves before class started. He pulled out his notebook and a pen, absently doodling on the margin of a page as the chatter around him began to blend into a low hum.

The final bell rang, signaling the official start of the day. The chatter in the room dimmed as Mr. Pearson cleared his throat. "Alright, class, let's get started. Open your textbooks to page 134."

Noah flipped his book open but continued to doodle, his mind drifting to scenes from his favorite movies. He imagined himself running alongside Indiana Jones, dodging traps and outsmarting villains in search of ancient artifacts. Or perhaps standing shoulder-to-shoulder with Luke Skywalker, lightsaber in hand, ready to take on the Empire and save the galaxy. They just didn't make movies like that anymore.

A gentle breeze rustled the leaves outside, catching his attention. He looked out the window to see the trees swaying, as if dancing to a song only they could hear. Birds flitted from branch to branch, free and unburdened.

"Harper," a stern voice cut through his reverie.

Noah blinked, turning his gaze to the front of the classroom. Mr. Pearson was staring directly at him, one eyebrow arched. The room had fallen silent; all eyes now focused on him.

"Yes?" Noah replied hesitantly.

"I asked if you would care to explain the significance of the steam engine in the Industrial Revolution."

Noah felt heat rise to his face. "Um… it… it was crucial because it allowed for more efficient transportation and manufacturing?"

"Good," Mr. Pearson said, though his tone suggested mild annoyance. "Please try to stay engaged."

"Sorry," Noah mumbled, sinking slightly in his seat.

A few snickers emanated from the back of the room. He didn't need to look to know who it was—Todd and his entourage.

Noah tightened his grip on his pen, his eyes fixed on his notebook as he shaded in the DeLorean he'd started earlier, pressing a little harder than necessary.

He felt a light nudge from his right. Glancing over, he caught Lily's quick, reassuring smile before she turned back to her notes. Noah let out a quiet breath he didn't realize he'd been holding. The tension in his shoulders eased just a bit.

The rest of the class proceeded without incident, Mr. Pearson delving deeper into the impacts of industrialization. Noah forced himself to jot down key points, though his mind still wandered.

When the bell finally rang, signaling the end of the period, Noah gathered his things quickly. As he stood to leave, Mr. Pearson called out.

"Mr. Harper, a word, please."

Noah froze mid-step, then cautiously made his way to the teacher's desk as the other students filed out.

"Yes, sir?"

Mr. Pearson adjusted his glasses, looking at him thoughtfully. "You're a bright student, Noah. Your test scores are solid—impressive, really. But I can't help but notice that you're often... somewhere else during lectures."

Noah shifted, the words sticking in his throat. "I… I guess I just have a lot on my mind," Noah admitted.

"We all do," Mr. Pearson replied, his tone softening slightly. "But part of learning is being present. If you're struggling with anything, or if there's anything you need help with, my door is always open."

"Thank you," Noah said, offering a faint smile.

Mr. Pearson studied him for a moment longer before returning a brief smile. "Good. Now, get on to your next class before you're late," he advised, turning back to the stack of papers in front of him.

Noah slipped into the crowded hallway. As he walked, he felt a familiar restlessness creeping in, a pull to be somewhere else, doing something more. He glanced out a nearby window as he walked past where sunlight spilled over the school lawn. For a moment, the world outside seemed bigger, freer.

The warning bell jolted him back to the moment. He let out a quiet sigh as he turned toward his next class, his thoughts settling as he fell into step with the crowd.

CHAPTER TWO

T he day passed in the usual blur of classes and routine, until he spotted her in his 4th period class. He had never seen her before. She was perched on the edge of a desk, laughing at something, sitting comfortably within a group of girls. Everything about her seemed to vibrate with life, from the way she tossed her hair to the casual confidence in her posture. Noah caught himself watching her for a second longer than he meant to.

And then, surprisingly, she looked his way.

Their eyes met for a split second before he quickly looked down, his cheeks warming. But not before he saw her smile—a quick, genuine flash of teeth and bright eyes that lingered even after he'd turned away.

Noah tried to refocus on the worksheet in front of him, a dull exercise on Shakespearean sonnets, but his concentration wavered. He snuck another glance, his eyes darting across the room like a nervous bird. The sound of her laugh—light, melodic—cut through the general classroom chatter, standing out like the first note of a song.

Mr. Cartwright cleared his throat at the front of the room, his balding head glinting under the fluorescent lights. "Let's focus, everyone. Shakespeare may be dead, but these grades are very much alive."

A few scattered chuckles rippled through the room, but Noah barely noticed. Who was she? Why hadn't he noticed her before?

He turned his attention back to his worksheet, forcing himself to focus. *Write your interpretation of the central theme of Sonnet 18.* His pen hovered over the page. Something about beauty and time? He scribbled an answer, but his thoughts kept drifting back to her. Her energy was magnetic, almost overwhelming in its brightness. It was the way she seemed completely at ease, as though she belonged everywhere she went.

The rest of the class felt like a blur. He kept sneaking glances, wondering if she'd look his way again. But she didn't, and by the time the bell rang, he'd convinced himself it was nothing. Just a random glance, an accidental meeting of eyes.

But later, during his free period, he found himself in a quiet corner of the library where he could pull out his sketchbook and lose himself in a world that didn't require eye contact or small talk. He had just flipped to a page, pencil hovering over the paper, when he sensed someone sliding into the seat across from him.

He looked up, startled, and saw her grinning at him from across the table.

"Well, hey there, stranger," she said, resting her chin in her hand. "Didn't mean to interrupt your intense drawing."

He blinked, momentarily thrown off balance. "Oh, um… it's not… I mean, I wasn't really…"

She laughed, a soft, amused sound that made him both flustered and oddly at ease. "I'm just kidding. I thought I'd find you here." She gestured to his notebook. "Can I see what you're working on?"

Noah hesitated, glancing down at his sketchbook. "It's… nothing really. Just some random stuff."

"Oh, come on," she said, leaning in with a mischievous glint in her eye. "Let me guess—you're drawing something really profound, like… the meaning of life?"

A small smile tugged at the corner of his mouth despite himself. "Not exactly. More like… plants. And trees."

"Nature. Nice." She leaned back, still grinning. "I could tell you were an artist."

He shifted uncomfortably, but there was something about her smile that made him feel… well, seen. And he wasn't sure how he felt about that.

"So, Noah," she continued, folding her arms on the table. "What's a guy like you doing hiding out here all by yourself?"

Noah blinked, caught off guard.

"How do you know my name?" he asked.

She raised an eyebrow, clearly amused. "You're in my English class. Mr. Cartwright calls on you, like, every other day. I'm pretty sure I've heard him say 'Harper' at least fifteen times this week."

"Oh," Noah said, feeling a little dumb.

She laughed again, her eyes sparkling. "You're funny, you know that?"

Noah blinked. Funny? No one had ever called him that before. Quiet, sure. Awkward, maybe. But funny? He wasn't sure what to make of it.

She nodded toward his sketchbook again. "Seriously, though. Can I see?"

He hesitated, but something about her felt genuine. Slowly, he turned the book around, showing her the rough outline of a sprawling tree with intricate branches.

"Wow," she said, leaning in for a closer look. "That's amazing. Do you draw a lot?"

"Sometimes," he said, his voice quieter now. "It's just... something I do to relax."

"Well, you're really good at it," she said, sitting back in her chair. "Like, way better than anything I could ever do."

Noah felt his cheeks warm, but her praise stirred something in him—a small, unfamiliar flicker of pride.

She nodded as if this made perfect sense. "You know what I think?" She leaned forward, eyes sparkling. "I think you could use a little more excitement in your life."

He blinked. "What do you mean?"

She leaned forward, her tone shifting from playful to serious. "Actually, I wanted to ask you something. I'm working on this project for Civics class, and I could use your help. It's a little... unconventional, but I think it could be fun. What do you think?"

Noah hesitated, his old instincts kicking in. But there was a part of him—the part she had somehow nudged awake—that was tempted.

"Um... what kind of project?" he asked cautiously.

"Oh, you'll see." She grinned, clearly loving the mystery. "It involves some creativity and maybe a bit of rule-breaking. But don't worry, nothing too illegal." She winked, and despite himself, Noah felt a small thrill at the idea.

After a beat, he found himself nodding. "All right. I'm in."

"Awesome!" She clapped her hands together, rising from the table, looking genuinely excited. "I'll find you after school and go over the details."

She turned to leave, but after a few steps, she paused and looked back over her shoulder. "Oh, by the way— I'm Riley." She flashed him one last smile.

She was perfect.

And with that, she was gone, leaving him with a strange feeling. He looked down at his sketchbook, her words lingering in his mind. Rule-breaking, huh?

The rest of the day felt a little lighter, though Noah couldn't quite pinpoint why. Maybe it was Riley's infectious energy, the way she seemed to draw him out of his own head without even trying. Or maybe it was the way she talked to him—not like he was invisible, not like he was some awkward guy she barely knew, but like he was someone worth listening to. Whatever it was, it stuck with him, a faint buzz of something he couldn't quite name.

As the hours ticked by, he caught himself glancing at the clock more than usual, willing the day to speed up. By the time the final bell rang, the anticipation humming in his chest was almost unbearable. He slung his backpack over one shoulder and wandered to his locker, moving with what he hoped was a casual stride.

The hallway buzzed with the familiar end-of-day chaos: lockers slamming, sneakers squeaking on the tile floor, snippets of hurried conversations echoing as students filtered toward the exits. Noah opened his locker, pulling out his books with an unusual level of care.

His eyes flicked down the hall as he slid a notebook into his bag. No sign of her yet. He adjusted his bag strap, then reorganized his books again, shifting them pointlessly just to have something to do. He didn't want to seem like he was waiting.

A couple of guys from his chemistry class walked past, laughing about something he didn't catch. A girl with a violin case hurried by, muttering about missing the bus. Minutes ticked by, the hallway growing quieter as the steady stream of students trickled to just a handful.

Still, Riley didn't appear.

Noah leaned back against the lockers. Maybe she'd forgotten. Or maybe something had come up. It wasn't like they'd made official plans, right? Maybe she hadn't meant it as seriously as he'd thought.

He frowned, the buzz of excitement that had carried him through the day dimming into something smaller. He pulled out his phone, checking the time as if that would make a difference. A few more students passed by, their voices echoing faintly in the empty hallway.

Noah sighed, pushing off the lockers while closing his own. He glanced down the corridor one last time. Still no Riley.

He let out a small sigh, adjusting the strap of his backpack before heading toward the library. Maybe he'd misunderstood. Maybe she wasn't serious about the project. Or maybe she'd just forgotten.

But when he reached the quiet corner where they'd met earlier, there she was, already setting up a table with an assortment of supplies: scissors, glue sticks, old magazines, and a stack of brightly colored construction paper.

"Thought you'd stand me up," she teased, grinning as he approached.

"Sorry," Noah said, though he wasn't entirely sure why. "I didn't know where we were meeting."

"Well, you're here now," she said, sliding into a seat. "Let's make some magic."

Noah felt a little out of his depth. Art projects weren't exactly his strong suit—he usually stuck to simpler, more structured assignments. But Riley's excitement was hard to resist.

"Okay," Riley began, leaning forward with her arms braced on the table. "So, I was thinking we could do something really different for this project. Like, instead of a boring poster or some PowerPoint slides, we could create a collage. Something dynamic. We could layer quotes and images from classic movies—give it a totally retro 80's vibe. What do you think?"

Noah blinked, surprised. "You... like 80's movies?"

Riley's grin widened. "Are you kidding me? I grew up on them. My mom and I used to have these movie nights where we'd watch movies like *Stand by Me* and *Raiders of the Lost Ark* on repeat. There's just something about the way those stories hit you."

He nodded slowly. "I know exactly what you mean. I have this old VHS player at home. And sometimes I'll play soundtracks from those movies. There's one from

Footloose that I've probably played a hundred times."

Riley's eyes lit up, and she let out an incredulous laugh. "No way! That's one of my all-time favorites! 'Let's Hear It for the Boy' is such a jam. Don't even get me started on young Kevin Bacon." She paused, her expression turning thoughtful. "You know, we could totally use that. 80's teen flicks, that raw coming-of-age energy—it would be perfect for this project."

Noah felt himself relaxing into the moment, the usual self-consciousness that often followed him fading away. Her enthusiasm was contagious, and he felt an unfamiliar thrill at the idea of collaborating on something creative. He smiled, leaning forward to meet her energy. "Okay, let's do it. Where do we start?"

Riley grabbed a blank sheet of paper and started sketching out a rough layout, her brow furrowed in concentration. "First, we'll need a strong centerpiece. Something that draws the eye and anchors the whole thing. Something iconic."

"Life moves pretty fast. If you don't stop and look around once in a while, you could miss it," Noah suggested without hesitation.

Riley's head shot up, her grin spreading ear to ear. "Yes! That's perfect. *Ferris Bueller's Day Off* is such a vibe."

Noah chuckled, feeling a flicker of pride. "We could build around that, layering it with images from other classics—like Molly Ringwald in *Pretty in Pink*."

Riley nodded eagerly, already flipping through one of the magazines. "And we should mix in some quotes that resonate, you know? Stuff that's meaningful, not just fluff. I'm thinking, 'Nobody puts Baby in a corner.' Or something from *The Breakfast Club*. What about, 'We're all pretty bizarre. Some of us are just better at hiding it'?"

"That's a good one," Noah agreed, his mind racing with possibilities. He grabbed another magazine and began flipping through the pages. "What if we also added some personal touches? Like, our own interpretations of these scenes. I can sketch out a few ideas to layer over the photos."

Riley paused mid-flip, looking up at him. "That's a great idea!" she said, then slid a blank piece of paper toward him. "Show me what you've got."

Noah hesitated for a moment, then reached for a pencil. He glanced at Riley, who was watching him with an encouraging smile, and let out a slow breath. As he started sketching, the lines came easily. He worked quickly, capturing the outline of a scene from *The Karate Kid*—a lone figure balanced in the crane kick pose atop a weathered post, the setting sun behind him casting a long shadow across the page.

When he finished, he slid the paper toward Riley without a word, his heart pounding slightly. She picked it up and studied it, her expression shifting from curiosity to delight.

"Noah," she said, her voice soft. "This is… really good. Like, wow. You've been holding out on me."

He let out a nervous laugh, scratching the back of his neck. "It's nothing special."

"It's incredible," she insisted, holding the sketch up to the light. "We're definitely using this. It's going front and center."

Her excitement was infectious, and Noah couldn't help but smile. For once, he didn't feel the need to downplay his efforts or brush off the compliment. Instead, he leaned into the moment, letting himself feel proud.

Their ideas clicked together like puzzle pieces, each suggestion sparking the next. Riley proposed layering vintage advertisements in the background for texture, while Noah came up with the idea of using colored thread to connect different elements, mimicking the lines of a movie reel. They laughed as they experimented, cutting out images and rearranging them on the page until the collage began to take shape.

At one point, Riley held up a pair of scissors, a mischievous glint in her eye. "Think we should find a pair of those old-timey 3D glasses? Add some dimension."

Noah laughed. "I don't think that's how 3D works."

"Fine," she said, grinning as she set the scissors down. "But I'm keeping that idea in my back pocket for the next project."

Hours seemed to pass in what felt like minutes. The library's quiet hum wrapped around them and formed a bubble where creativity flowed freely and conversation came easily. Noah couldn't remember the last time he'd felt so relaxed, so present.

"Hey," Riley said suddenly. She leaned forward, resting her chin on her hand as she studied him. "You know, you're a lot more creative than you let on."

Noah glanced up, caught off guard by the warmth in her voice. "What do you mean?"

"I mean," she said, her smile softening, "you've got all this talent and all these ideas, and yet, you keep it to yourself. Why?"

He hesitated, the question catching him off guard. "I guess... I don't know. I didn't think anyone would care."

"Well, I care," Riley said firmly. "And I'm pretty sure anyone who sees this is going to care too."

Her words hung in the air, settling over him like a warm blanket. He felt a flicker of something unfamiliar—acceptance, maybe, or the quiet thrill of being truly seen. For once, he didn't look away. Instead, he met her gaze and offered a small, genuine smile.

"Guess I've just been waiting for the right project," he said.

Riley laughed, "Well, you've got one now."

As they leaned over the table, rearranging the final pieces of their collage, Noah realized how different this felt. Working with Riley wasn't awkward or forced—it was easy, like they'd fallen into a rhythm without even trying. For the first time in a long while, he wasn't second-guessing himself or overthinking every word. He could just be... him.

Later that evening, Noah was back in his bedroom, the dim light of his desk lamp casting a soft glow over his workspace. His sketchbook lay open in front of him, the half-finished drawing staring back at him. It was a detailed piece—a set of old Hollywood hands holding a clapboard, surrounded by swirling film reels that seemed to leap off the page. He picked up his pencil, twirling it between his fingers as his eyes traced the lines he'd already drawn.

The room was quiet except for the faint hum of his computer and the soft creaks of the house settling around him. His desk was cluttered but comfortably so: a stack of books teetering precariously on one side, an empty coffee mug next to his eraser, and a tangle of earbuds he kept meaning to untangle.

Noah leaned forward, adding shading to the hands in his drawing. The clapboard bore the iconic "Scene 1, Take 1" written in bold letters, and he carefully darkened the edges to give it depth. As he worked, his mind drifted back to the library, to the easy flow of conversation with Riley. He'd felt different there, sitting across from her, bouncing ideas back and forth without the usual overthinking that often paralyzed him.

He paused, setting the pencil down and flexing his fingers. Normally, he'd second-guess every word, replay every moment in his head, picking apart what he could've said differently or better. But today? Today had been... easy. Effortless. Riley had a way of drawing him out, of making him forget the walls he usually kept so carefully in place. He wasn't sure how she did it—whether it was her enthusiasm, her confidence, or just her being Riley— but he realized, with a small flicker of surprise, that he liked it. He liked the version of himself he saw when he was around her.

Shaking off the thought, he turned his attention back to his drawing. He reached for his eraser, gently rubbing away a smudge near the edge of the clapboard. The sound of pencil against paper filled the room as he added more detail to the film reels, giving them a sense of motion.

The sketch was coming to life, and with each stroke, he felt a quiet sense of accomplishment building in his chest.

After a while, Noah sat back in his chair, letting the pencil drop onto the desk. He glanced around his room, taking in the familiar surroundings. His bed was unmade, the comforter half-draped over the side, and his dresser was cluttered with random knickknacks: an old ticket stub from a concert, a model car he'd built in middle school, and a framed photo of his family at the beach.

He stood up, stretching his arms above his head, and wandered over to the window. The sky outside was almost dark now, streaked with hues of deep blue and faint orange as the last light of the day faded. He pushed the window open slightly, letting the cool evening air seep into the room. It carried with it the faint scent of grass and the distant hum of a neighbor's television.

Turning away from the window, he wandered over to his bookshelf, his fingers trailing along the spines of well-worn books and a few neglected ones he'd always meant to read. He pulled out a thin, tattered volume—an old book of movie trivia his mom had given him years ago. Flipping through the pages, he smiled at the photos and fun facts scattered throughout. A caption under a photo of Robin Williams in *Dead Poets Society* caught his eye: "Carpe diem. Seize the day, boys. Make your lives extraordinary."

"Perfect for the collage," he muttered to himself, setting the book down on his desk. He made a mental note to show Riley the quote tomorrow.

His stomach growled, pulling him from his thoughts. He glanced at the clock—it was later than he'd realized.

With a sigh, he made his way to the kitchen, his socks sliding slightly on the hardwood floor as he padded down the hallway. The house was quiet, his parents already upstairs. He rummaged through the fridge, pulling out leftover spaghetti from dinner and popping it into the microwave.

As the microwave hummed, he leaned against the counter, staring absentmindedly at the blinking numbers. He thought about the way Riley had laughed earlier, how genuine and full of excitement she'd been when they talked about old movies. The memory made him smile.

When the microwave beeped, he grabbed the plate and a fork, heading back to his room. He balanced the plate on the edge of his desk, careful not to spill, and took a few bites as he flipped through his sketchbook. The drawing of the clapboard was nearly done, but he felt like it needed something more—maybe a background, or some color to make it pop.

Setting his fork down, he picked up a colored pencil and began shading the reels with soft grays, blending the edges to create a metallic sheen. The process was calming, each movement of the pencil grounding him. He found himself getting lost in the details, the minutes slipping away as the image came to life under his hand.

When he finally set the pencil down, Noah leaned back in his chair, studying the finished piece. The clapboard was bold and striking, the film reels swirling around it like a frame. He felt a pang of satisfaction, the kind that came from seeing an idea fully realized. It wasn't perfect—he could already spot a few places where the lines weren't as clean as he wanted—but it was his.

Before bed, Noah sat on the edge of his mattress, staring out the window at the now fully dark sky. He thought about the day—about the ease he'd felt with Riley. It was a small thing, working on a project together, but it had opened something inside him. A door, maybe, or a window. A chance to let himself be seen.

And for the first time, it didn't feel terrifying. It felt exciting.

As he reached over to turn off his desk lamp, his eyes fell on the sketchbook resting on the desk. He smiled to himself. Maybe he didn't have to be invisible. Maybe, with a little courage and a friend like Riley, he could take up just a little more space in his own life.

With that quiet realization warming his chest, he pulled the blankets over himself and closed his eyes. The weight of the day lifted, replaced by a growing sense of possibility. The darkness of the room felt less like an end and more like a beginning.

And as he drifted off to sleep, a single thought lingered in his mind: *I can do this.*

CHAPTER THREE

N oah awoke that morning feeling lighter, as if something had shifted deep inside. He swung his legs out of bed and shuffled toward the mirror above his dresser.

He paused, catching his reflection in the early morning light. His hair was sticking up in the usual unruly way, and his hoodie from the night before hung off the back of his desk chair in a crumpled heap. But what caught his attention most was the small, unfamiliar smile tugging at the corners of his mouth. It wasn't forced or fleeting, as if his face had finally relaxed after years of holding tension he hadn't even realized was there.

Turning away, Noah opened the top drawer of his dresser, rifling through an assortment of folded t-shirts until he found one that felt right—simple, but not too plain. He pulled it over his head, the soft cotton cool against his skin, and gave himself one last glance in the mirror. It wasn't a big change, but there was something satisfying about seeing himself put together, ready to face the day.

Satisfied, Noah grabbed his phone from the nightstand and slipped it into his pocket before heading downstairs. The smell of fresh coffee drifted up as he made his way to the kitchen, whistling softly. His mom stood at the counter, sorting through a small pile of mail, a mug in her other hand.

She glanced up as he entered, her sharp eyes softening with a smile. "You're looking unusually chipper this morning. What's up?"

Noah paused, pouring a bowl of cereal. "What? I'm not allowed to be in a good mood?"

His dad lowered his newspaper, peering at him over the rim of his mug. "You can, but it's suspicious."

Noah rolled his eyes, focusing on his cereal. "It's nothing, okay? I just... met someone cool yesterday. That's all."

His mom set the mail down, her interest piqued. "Oh? A girl someone?"

Noah shrugged, not looking up. "Yeah, I guess. We talked for a bit in the library. It was nice."

His dad leaned back in his chair, smirking. "Nice, huh? That's a glowing review. What'd you talk about?"

"Stuff," Noah muttered, suddenly aware of the heat creeping up his neck.

"Stuff," his dad repeated. "Riveting."

His mom shot his dad a look, then turned back to Noah with a softer expression. "Well, that's great, honey. It's always nice to meet new people. I'm glad it put you in a good mood."

His dad raised his mug in mock toast. "Absolutely. Meeting someone equals no follow-up questions. Got it."

"Thank you," Noah said pointedly.

"Don't let us ruin your vibe, or whatever you kids call it these days. Just don't forget your lunch," he said, nodding toward the counter where a brown paper bag sat neatly folded.

"I won't," Noah said, slinging his backpack over one shoulder and grabbing the bag.

"Have a good one, kiddo," his mom called after him as he headed toward the door.

"Yeah, knock 'em dead," his dad added. "And remember, when you ace another test, it's okay to let us know."

Noah laughed lightly, shaking his head as he opened the door. "I'll keep that in mind."

As Noah started down the driveway, he felt a small flicker of something unfamiliar but welcome—a sense of pride in himself. It wasn't overwhelming, and it wasn't even fully formed, but it was there.

By the time he slid into his seat in third period, Noah's head rested heavily in the palm of his hand as he stared blankly at the chalkboard at the front of the classroom. The once-clean surface was now a chaotic maze of dates, maps, and bullet points—Mrs. Grayson's meticulous notes on European colonialism. She stood beside the board, pointer in hand, her tweed skirt and matching blazer giving her the stern appearance of someone who took Economics very, very seriously. Her silver-framed glasses perched on the bridge of her nose, catching the light every time she turned her head. "...and it's important to understand how the mercantile policies of the 17th century laid the groundwork for modern economics," she droned, her voice a steady monotone that seemed to sap the energy from the room. The rhythm of her speech was as predictable as the ticking of the old clock above the door. Each word blending into the next without inflection or pause.

Noah could feel his eyelids growing heavier with each passing minute. The fluorescent lights above buzzed softly, adding to the hypnotic effect of Mrs. Grayson's lecture. They cast a cold, artificial light that washed out the colors in the room, making everything appear slightly faded. He glanced around the room; a few students were diligently taking notes, their pens moving in a synchronized dance across their notebooks. But most seemed just as disengaged as he was. To his left, a girl was stealthily texting under her desk, her fingers moving rapidly over the screen while her eyes flicked up occasionally to feign attention. To his right, a guy was nodding off, his head bobbing precariously with each dip, only to jerk awake momentarily before starting the cycle anew.

In the far corner of the classroom, slouched in his seat with a lazy smirk, was Todd Benson, the school's notorious bully and self-appointed "king" of the junior class. Todd had a permanent scowl etched into his face, a thick ring piercing his eyebrow and a set of gleaming silver rings across his knuckles that flashed menacingly under the fluorescent lights. With a single look, Todd could make the hallway clear, the crowds parting to avoid his merciless taunts and rough shoves. He'd made it his mission to make life uncomfortable for anyone he considered an easy target—and Noah was a favorite.

Out of the corner of his eye, Noah caught Todd staring at him. With a quiet sigh, Noah looked down at his open notebook. The top half of the page contained a few scattered notes. His handwriting, usually neat, had become lazy scrawls, the letters leaning into one another as if they too were succumbing to boredom. The handwriting grew sloppier as it went down the page, eventually giving way to a sketch that consumed the rest of the space. An electric guitar was taking shape under his pen—a sleek Gibson Les Paul.

But before he could get lost in the sketch, a paper wad flew across the classroom, bouncing off his head and landing on his desk. A snicker followed. Noah didn't have to look to know it was Todd.

Noah clenched his jaw but refused to respond. His gaze drifted out the window beside him. The late morning sun filtered through the branches of the large oak tree just outside, casting dappled patterns of light and shadow on the floor. A gentle breeze rustled the leaves, causing flecks of sunlight to dance across his desk. For a moment, he imagined he could hear the whispering of the wind over Mrs. Grayson's voice, the rustling leaves forming a natural symphony that beckoned him to a world beyond these walls.

Noah let his thoughts wander. The sounds of the classroom faded, replaced by distant echoes of city life—the hum of traffic, the murmur of a crowd, the pulsing beat of music. The smell of chalk and old paper gave way to imagined scents of asphalt after rain and the electrifying aroma of excitement.

Suddenly, the beige walls and sterile fluorescent lights began to dissolve around him. Colors burst forth, vibrant and electric. Neon hues painted the world in shades of magenta, cyan, and electric blue. He blinked, and the world transformed.

He was now standing in the middle of a bustling city street at night. Towering skyscrapers surrounded him, their windows aglow with neon signs. Massive billboards displayed larger-than-life images of rock stars and sleek sports cars. The reflections danced in puddles on the wet pavement, creating a kaleidoscope of color that seemed to pulse with the beat of the city.

Noah looked down at himself. Gone were his worn jeans and faded denim jacket. Instead, he wore a black leather jacket, the collar turned up just so. Underneath, a vintage AC/DC tee clung to his frame, the faded *Highway to Hell* logo hinting at countless concerts and years of wear. The crackled letters and worn graphic spoke of a time when rock was raw and unapologetic. His hair was tousled, styled in that perfect blend of carelessness and cool. He could feel the metal rings on his fingers and a chain hanging from his belt loop. Slung across his back was the Les Paul from his sketchbook—only now, it was real, solid, and weighty. The strap was studded, and the body of the guitar gleamed under the city lights.

He smirked, confidence surging through him. "Noah *'Danger'* Harper," he said aloud, testing the name. It rolled off his tongue with a satisfying edge, embodying the rebellious spirit he felt coursing through his veins.

The sidewalk around him was filled with people. As Noah began to stride forward, they turned to look at him, eyes filled with recognition and admiration. A group pointed excitedly, while others whispered among themselves.

"Hey, it's Noah!" someone shouted.

"Rock the stage tonight, Danger!" another called out,

giving him a thumbs-up. A few fans rushed forward, holding out memorabilia for him to sign.

He nodded in acknowledgment, the corners of his mouth lifting into a confident grin. The pulsing rhythm of *Another One Bites the Dust* by Queen filled the air, the synthesized bassline propelling him forward. The beat matched his heartbeat, each step in perfect sync with the music. The energy was palpable, electrifying.

Up ahead, the glowing lights of a club beckoned. The sign above the entrance flickered "The Electric Pulse" in bold neon letters, the script stylized with jagged edges that resembled lightning bolts. The building itself seemed to throb with the beat of the music emanating from within.

As he approached, a hulking bouncer in dark sunglasses and an impeccably tailored suit stood guard at the door. The man's expression was impassive, but as Noah drew near, he stepped aside with a respectful nod.

"Evening, Mr. Harper," the bouncer said in a deep baritone that resonated over the ambient noise.

"Thanks, Gary," Noah replied smoothly, clapping him on the shoulder as he passed.

Inside, the club was a sensory explosion. Strobe lights flashed in time with the music, casting the crowd in alternating shades of color and shadow. Beams of light shot across the room, intersecting in a dazzling display overhead. People danced freely, lost in the rhythm. The floor was illuminated with patterns that shifted and swirled beneath their feet.

Noah weaved through the crowd, the sea of bodies parting effortlessly before him. Whispers and cheers followed in his wake.

"He's here!"

"Can't wait for the show!"

"You're gonna kill it tonight, Danger!"

He felt a surge of adrenaline. This was where he belonged—center stage, the focal point of energy and admiration. The anticipation was electric, each cheer fueling his excitement.

A spotlight snapped on, illuminating the stage at the far end of the club. There it was—a microphone waiting just for him, bathed in a halo of light. The band was already assembled—figures shrouded in mist, their features indistinct but their instruments gleaming under the lights. The drummer twirled his sticks, the bassist adjusted his amp, and the keyboardist ran fingers over the keys in a silent rehearsal.

As Noah took the stage, the crowd's roar intensified—a wave of sound that washed over him. He swung the guitar around, settling it against his hip. Grabbing the mic, he felt the cool metal under his fingers.

"Are you ready?" he asked, his voice amplified over the roaring crowd. It echoed, reverberating off the walls and filling every corner of the club.

The audience erupted in cheers, their collective excitement washing over him like a wave. Hands reached out toward him, faces alight with anticipation and adoration.

He nodded to the drummer, who counted off with a tap of his sticks—one, two, three, four. The music exploded into life—a driving beat, soaring synths, and a guitar riff that set his fingers ablaze.

Noah launched into the song, his voice strong and clear, carrying the melody effortlessly.

"Chasing the horizon, never looking back,
A fire in our hearts, burning through the cracks.
This is our anthem, our battle cry,
We'll take the leap—don't ask why."

The lyrics poured out of him, full of defiance and yearning. He moved across the stage, engaging with the audience, his energy infectious. The guitar felt like an extension of himself as he leaned out over the edge of the stage, strumming with fervor.

The crowd sang along, their voices merging with his:

"Run with the wind, let it guide your way,
Tear down the walls, don't let fear stay.
We'll rise like the sun, unstoppable light,
This is our moment—we own the night."

The sound swelled, the room alive with the force of the music. As the song reached its peak, Noah ripped into a guitar solo. His fingers flew across the fretboard.

The lights swirled around him—reds, blues, and purples intertwining in a dazzling display. A spotlight tracked his movements, highlighting the intensity of his performance. The crowd erupted in cheers, their hands in the air.

"We'll keep on running, no chains to bind,
A path unknown, but it's ours to find.
We're chasing dreams, we'll never fall—
Together we'll rise above it all."

The final chorus roared, the crowd singing every word in unison. Noah let the energy of the moment wash over him. He felt weightless, invincible, like nothing in the world could touch him.

Faces in the crowd blurred together, all eyes fixed on him. He could see their expressions—awed, inspired. They were with him, part of this shared moment. Sweat glistened on his brow, but he paid it no mind. Every sense was heightened, every emotion amplified.

"This is where I'm meant to be," he thought. The realization filled him with a profound sense of purpose.

But then, something shifted. Like a record scratch halting a song, the vibrant colors began to fade. The neon lights dimmed, the music grew muffled, distant. The crowd's cheers echoed as if from far away, and the energy dissipated like smoke. The stage lights flickered, and the band members became shadowy figures before disappearing altogether.

Confusion flickered across Noah's face. "Wait, what's happening?" he murmured, reaching out as if to grasp the fading scene. He tried to strum his guitar, but his fingers met only air. The weight of the instrument vanished, leaving him feeling strangely empty.

A voice cut through the haze—a distant, insistent call tinged with irritation.

"Noah Harper!"

He blinked, and suddenly he was back—seated once again in Mrs. Grayson's classroom. The walls were back to their dull beige, the fluorescent lights casting a stark glow. His classmates were staring at him with amusement. The ambient noises of the classroom flooded back in.

Mrs. Grayson stood at the front of the room, arms crossed over her chest, her brow furrowed in exasperation. Her eyes bore into him.

"Would you care to join us here in reality, Mr. Harper?" she asked pointedly.

Noah's face flushed a deep shade of crimson. "Uh, sorry," he mumbled, sitting up straighter in his seat. He realized his fingers were still curled as if holding an imaginary guitar. He quickly lowered his hands, clasping them together to hide his embarrassment.

A few students snickered.

He glanced down at his notebook. The drawing of the electric guitar stared back at him, suddenly seeming juvenile.

Mrs. Grayson sighed. "If I catch you drifting off again, you'll be taking a trip to the principal's office," she said, her tone leaving no room for argument. With that, she turned back to the board and continued her lecture, pointing to a map of trade routes.

Noah nodded, swallowing hard. "Yes, ma'am," he mumbled softly. He could feel the lingering gazes of his classmates slowly dissipating as they returned their focus to the lesson.

He took a deep breath to steady himself. The vividness of the daydream lingered at the edges of his consciousness—the feel of the guitar, the heat of the stage lights, the roar of the crowd. It had felt so real, so tangible. The abrupt return to reality left him feeling disoriented.

But now, under the harsh glare of the classroom lights, it all seemed so distant. He could still hear the faint echo of the music in his mind, but it was fading fast. The room felt colder, the colors duller.

Determined to shake off the lingering embarrassment, he flipped to a new page in his notebook and began jotting down the lyrics that had formed in his mind.

The bell rang suddenly, jolting Noah from his thoughts. Chairs scraped against the linoleum floor as students began to pack up their belongings. The atmosphere shifted instantly with chatter and the rustling of papers.

"Don't forget to read chapters five and six for tomorrow," Mrs. Grayson called out over the din. "There will be a quiz." She began erasing the board, the chalk dust forming a small cloud.

As he walked down the hallway toward his next class, Noah reached into his pocket and pulled out his headphones. Placing them over his ears, he selected "Everybody Wants to Rule the World" by Tears for Fears on his phone.

Just as he was starting to settle into the comfort of his own world, someone blocked his path. Noah looked up to see Todd standing in front of him, a smug grin stretching across his face. Todd's posse lingered nearby, exchanging knowing glances as they waited for whatever spectacle Todd had in mind.

"Well, if it isn't the Space Cadet," Todd sneered, loud enough for anyone nearby to hear. Noah felt the heat rise to his face. Keeping his eyes down, he tried to step around Todd, hoping he could just slide by. But Todd shifted to block him, crossing his arms.

"What's the rush?" Todd asked, smirking. He jabbed a thumb toward Noah's headphones. "What are you listening to? Something lame, right?"

Noah was used to Todd's jabs, but today they grated more than usual. He could feel eyes on him, a few students pretending not to look while obviously taking in every word.

Todd's hand shot out, plucking the headphone cord right from Noah's hand. He yanked the cord, unplugging it from Noah's phone, causing the music to cut off abruptly.

"Hey!" Noah protested, reaching for the headphones, but Todd held them out of reach, dangling them just above Noah's head. "Give them back, Todd."

Todd pulled back, laughing as he dangled the headphones in front of his friends. "Chill out, Harper. No need to get all worked up." His grin turned ominous. "Or are you gonna cry about it?"

The crowd around them seemed to grow. Noah forced himself to breathe. He knew that any sign of frustration would only feed Todd's taunts, but it was hard to hold back. He glanced over at Todd's friends, who were snickering, clearly enjoying the show. The words he wanted to say buzzed in his mind, but he swallowed them down.

Todd stepped closer, his voice cutting through the ambient noise. "You know, Harper, it's no wonder nobody wants to hang out with you. You're always off in your little world, like you're too good for the rest of us. Newsflash—you're not."

Noah swallowed the lump rising in his throat, clenching his fists.

"Seriously, Todd," Noah said, his voice low and tight.

"Give. Them. Back."

Todd's friends exchanged glances, one of them letting out a low whistle. "Ooh, Harper's getting mad," one of them muttered.

Todd's grin widened. "Fine," he said, but instead of handing the headphones back, he flung them across the hallway. They hit the lockers with a *clink* before falling to the floor.

"Oops," Todd said, shrugging dramatically. "My bad."

Noah didn't even look at him. He turned and crouched to pick up the headphones, his hands trembling slightly as he checked for damage.

"See you around, Harper," Todd said. With that, he walked off, his posse trailing behind him, their laughter echoing down the hallway.

Noah stood there, clutching his headphones, feeling the anger and embarrassment roiling inside him. He put them back on, pressing play with more force than necessary, and took a deep breath, willing himself to let the music smooth over the jagged edges of his frustration.

He continued down the hall without looking up. He replayed the interaction in his head, wishing he could have said something clever or brave. Instead, he felt the sting of Todd's words, lingering like an unwelcome reminder of the boundary between the world he dreamed of and the one he was stuck in.

The noise of students and slamming lockers faded behind him as he turned into the cafeteria. The smell of school pizza and mystery casserole hung in the air. He hesitated at the entrance, unsure where to go, scanning the crowd with a vague sense of detachment.

Noah found himself searching for Riley. He found her at the back of the cafeteria, leaning against the wall. She waved him over with a small smile, and they silently slipped outside.

They found a spot under a tree. Riley plopped down on the grass, crossing her legs as she looked up at the sky with a contemplative expression. For a moment, they sat in comfortable silence, each lost in their own thoughts.

Finally, Riley broke the quiet. "You ever feel like you're supposed to be someone, even when you don't really feel like that person?"

Noah looked at her, surprised by the question. "Yeah... all the time, actually," he replied quietly. "Yeah... like people already decided who you are, so you just go along with it." He hesitated, then added, "I guess it's easier than trying to prove them wrong."

She nodded while tracing a pattern in the dirt with her finger. "People expect me to be this... happy, confident girl. The one who has it all together, who's always there for everyone. And I guess I play the part because it's just easier that way." Her voice softened, almost like she was sharing a secret. "But sometimes, I feel like I'm just pretending."

Noah's chest tightened. He'd never considered that Riley, of all people, might feel the pressure to keep up appearances. "I never would have guessed," he admitted. "You seem so... sure of yourself."

Riley let out a small laugh, but there was no humor in it. "That's the trick, right? You act like you're okay, and eventually people believe it. And if they believe it, maybe you start believing it too."

They both fell silent, the words settling heavily between them. "I get that. Like, if people don't see me, they won't expect anything from me. But it gets lonely after a while."

Riley looked up at him. "So why did you agree to work with me on my project?"

He paused, considering her question. "I guess... because you didn't let me hide. You saw me. And you didn't expect me to be anything else." The words came out quietly, but the honesty in them was raw, vulnerable.

Riley smiled, a real, genuine smile that reached her eyes. "You know, for a guy who tries to hide, you're pretty amazing when you let yourself be seen."

They sat there, their confessions hanging in the air, binding them together in a shared understanding. In that moment, Noah felt an unspoken connection between them, a silent promise that they didn't have to pretend around each other. It was a rare and beautiful thing, and he felt his heart swell with a quiet gratitude.

CHAPTER FOUR

N oah's alarm went off. He lay there for a moment, staring at the ceiling, feeling a strange combination of nerves and resolve swirling in his chest. The vulnerability he'd shared with Riley the day before had opened something inside him, something that had been locked away for so long he'd nearly forgotten it was there. It was a glimmer of confidence, a hint of belief that maybe he didn't have to stay invisible forever.

As he got out of bed, a thought struck him—he wanted to go all-in. He wanted to show himself what it would feel like to fully embrace his own uniqueness.

He opened his closet and stared at the usual lineup: plain t-shirts, jeans, and a couple of hoodies, all in muted tones. Today, he wanted to try something different. Today, he wanted to be seen.

His fingers brushed over a deep green button-down shirt he'd shoved toward the back of his closet—a gift from his aunt last year. He'd never worn it, thinking it was too attention-grabbing. But now, he pulled it out, slipping it on and rolling up the sleeves just the way he'd seen other guys do, the ones who seemed so cool.

For a second, he hesitated, feeling the familiar tug of doubt. But then he thought of Riley, of her unapologetic way of moving through the world. If she could do it, maybe he could too.

After a final glance in the mirror, he grabbed his backpack and headed downstairs. As he stepped into the kitchen, his mom glanced up, her eyebrows raising in pleasant surprise.

"Well, look at you!" she exclaimed, a smile spreading across her face. "New look?"

Noah shrugged, trying to play it off, but he felt the warmth of her approval settle over him. "Just… thought I'd try something different."

"It suits you," she said softly, her voice laced with pride. "You look great, Noah."

At the table, his dad sat behind a fortress of newspaper, his coffee mug steaming in his hand. He peered over the top with a grin. "Hey, bud. TGIF!"

Noah stopped mid-step, narrowing his eyes. "No. Just no."

His dad set the paper down, feigning outrage. "What? It's Friday!"

"By using phrases no one's said since the nineteen hundreds," Noah said, pouring himself some orange juice.

"Fine. Would you prefer YOLO? I can be modern."

Noah stared at him, glass halfway to his lips. "You saying 'YOLO' is actually worse."

His mom glanced over her shoulder, amused. "If we don't stop him now, he's going to start dabbing."

"Not true," his dad protested. "That requires getting out of this chair."

Noah shook his head. "You're lucky this is too early for me to process how cringe this is."

"Cringe?" His dad put down his coffee. "What's next, calling me a boomer?"

His mom smirked. "Enthusiasm at 7 AM? That's suspicious behavior."

"Thank you," Noah said, pointing at her.

His dad leaned back in his chair, undeterred. "You'll miss this one day, y'know. My dad jokes are part of the fabric of this household."

"Pretty sure that fabric is polyester," Noah muttered, pouring himself a bowl of cereal.

He grabbed a spoon and sat, eyeing his dad as he took the first bite. His mom stifled a laugh as she leaned back against the counter.

"Cutting it close today, huh?" his mom said glancing at the microwave clock.

"Barely," Noah muttered, spoon halfway to his mouth. "I've got plenty of time."

His dad lowered the paper just enough to give Noah a skeptical look. "You've got the urgency of a sloth."

"Sloths are efficient," Noah said between bites.

His dad chuckled. "Efficient at doing nothing. That's what you're going for?"

"Exactly," Noah said "It's an art more than science".

His dad shook his head, folding the newspaper. "This kid's aiming for gold in the Procrastination Olympics. Impressive."

Noah rolled his eyes, standing up and taking his bowl to the sink. "You should start a sitcom."

"Not a bad idea," his dad said, tapping his coffee mug on the table. "We'll call it *Why Is My Teenager So Difficult?*"

"Catchy," Noah said dryly, grabbing his lunch bag from the counter.

As he stepped outside, his dad called after him, "Go knock 'em dead, kid! And remember—efficient like a sloth!"

Noah smiled, shaking his head as the door clicked shut behind him, the cool morning air brushing his face.

The shrill ring of the bell signaled the end of chemistry class, echoing through the corridors like a starter pistol. Noah methodically packed his textbook and notebook into his backpack, waiting for the initial rush of students to filter out before he stepped into the hallway. The moment he crossed the threshold, he was enveloped by the tide of bodies moving in every direction, the crush of energy that followed every transition between classes.

He kept his gaze fixed on the scuffed linoleum floor, his sneakers navigating the familiar path to his next class. Around him, the cacophony of high school life surged.

Suddenly he felt a sudden warmth envelop him. Two arms wrapped around his shoulders from behind, a soft weight pressing against his back. The scent of jasmine and something sweet—vanilla, maybe—filled his senses.

"There you are!" came the familiar, cheerful voice. Her laughter bubbled just above the din of the hallway, rising like a melody above the background noise.

Noah's heart skipped a beat, and despite himself, a small smile tugged at the corner of his mouth. Riley had a way of bursting into his world like sunlight streaming through a window—unexpected and warm, with an energy that seemed to lift everything around her.

He turned his head slightly, catching a glimpse of her mischievous eyes peeking over his shoulder. She grinned, her face alight with the kind of joy that made it impossible not to smile back, even if just a little.

Riley released her embrace and moved to stand beside him, slipping her arm comfortably through his. Her bangle bracelets jingled softly with the movement, adding a rhythm to their interaction, and Noah noticed how her presence seemed to brighten everything around him.

"Noah," she said playfully, "I've come to whisk you away."

Today, Riley was dressed in her usual eclectic style— a flowing, oversized cardigan with bold geometric patterns that added a hint of bohemian flair. Her hair, a cascade of auburn curls, framed her face in a way that made her look like she belonged on an album cover, effortlessly cool but with an edge of wildness.

He raised an eyebrow, eyeing her warily. "Whisk me away where?"

"You'll see," she replied cryptically, grabbing his hand before he could protest. Her warm fingers intertwined with his. There was something comforting about the way she held on to him.

"Riley, I have class," he began, but she was already pulling him forward, her steps light and confident.

"Relax! We've got a few minutes," she insisted with a breezy nonchalance. "Plenty of time."

He allowed himself to be led through the throng of students as Riley expertly navigated the crowded hallway. Noah saw the curious glances of others as they passed by.

"People are staring," he muttered under his breath, feeling self-conscious under the weight of so many eyes.

"Let them," she said breezily, shrugging off the attention like it didn't matter.

They emerged into the open air of the courtyard, the cool breeze a welcome contrast to the stuffy hallways. The sky was a clear expanse of blue, the sun casting a warm glow over the campus.

Riley released his hand and spun around to face him, her arms wide open as if embracing the world. "Isn't it a beautiful day?" she exclaimed with a grin that seemed to radiate joy.

Noah shoved his hands into his jacket pockets, a small smile playing on his lips. "It is," he agreed. "But I still don't know what I'm supposed to be looking at."

She stepped closer, her expression shifting to something more thoughtful. Her eyes met his, and for a moment, she looked almost serious. "I'm not just talking about today, Noah," she said, her voice softer now. "I'm talking about everything. Life, possibilities, whatever's out there waiting for you. You just have to be open to seeing it."

He felt a flicker of something—hope? Excitement? He wasn't sure. "What if I don't know how?" he asked softly.

She smiled gently. "Then that's where I come in. Think of me as your *personal tour guide to the extraordinary*."

He laughed. "That's quite a title."

"Well, I take my job very seriously," she replied with

a wink, her playful demeanor back in full force.

As they stood there for a moment, Noah felt a strange sense of calm wash over him.

"Why me?" he blurted out before he could stop himself.

Riley looked puzzled. "What do you mean?"

He hesitated. "Why did you choose me to... you know, be friends with?"

She tilted her head, considering him thoughtfully. "Maybe I see something in you that you don't see in yourself," she said finally. "Plus, you're a good listener. Most people just wait for their turn to talk."

He felt his cheeks warm. "Maybe I'm just not great at small talk."

She laughed lightly. "That's okay. I prefer big talk anyway—dreams, fears, the meaning of life. All that deep stuff."

"Well, when you put it that way…"

She grinned, giving him a light shove. "See? You're more interesting than you give yourself credit for."

The bell rang, its sharp tone cutting through the air.

"Looks like our time's up," Noah noted, glancing back toward the building.

Riley shrugged nonchalantly. "Time is relative."

He raised an eyebrow. "Try telling that to Mr. Daniels when we're late for math."

She waved a dismissive hand. "I have a foolproof plan."

"Oh really?"

"Absolutely," she declared confidently. "Just follow my lead."

As they headed back inside, Riley launched into a story about her latest adventure—something about sneaking into an open mic night and nearly getting on stage before security intervened.

"You did what?" Noah asked, incredulous.

She laughed. "I know, right? It was exhilarating! You should come with me next time."

He shook his head. "I don't think I'm cut out for that kind of excitement."

"Nonsense," she said, nudging him with her elbow. "You might surprise yourself."

They reached the door to math class, the hallway now quiet as most students were already seated. Riley paused, turning to him with a conspiratorial smile.

"Ready?" she whispered.

"For what?" he whispered back.

She didn't answer, simply pushed open the door and strode in confidently. Noah followed a step behind, trying to appear inconspicuous.

Mr. Daniels looked up from his desk, his expression stern. "How kind of you to join us."

"Sorry, Mr. D," Noah said embarrassingly.

Mr. Daniels regarded him for a moment before sighing. "Take your seat. Page 142, we're discussing quadratic equations."

They slipped into their seats, and Noah shot Riley a look. She winked in response.

As the lesson progressed, Noah found it hard to focus. His mind kept replaying their conversation in the courtyard. Riley's words echoed in his thoughts: There's more to all of this, but you've got to be willing to see it.

He glanced over at her. She was diligently taking notes, her brow furrowed in concentration. Sensing his gaze, she looked up and offered a small smile.

"Need help?" she mouthed silently.

He shook his head, returning the smile. Maybe she was right. Maybe there was more to life than the quiet existence he'd carved out for himself.

When the class ended, Riley packed up her things and turned to him. "Walk with me?" she asked.

"Sure," he agreed, slinging his backpack over his shoulder. They navigated the bustling hallways once more.

"So, any plans after school?" she inquired.

He shrugged. "Not really. Just the usual—homework, maybe watch a movie."

She made a face. "Sounds thrilling."

He smiled. "Not all of us have your flair for the dramatic."

She tapped her chin thoughtfully. "Well, what if I told you I had something exciting to share?"

He raised an eyebrow. "Should I be worried?"

"Only if you're allergic to fun," she teased.

He considered her offer. "Alright, I'm intrigued. What is it?"

She wagged a finger. "Uh-uh, not here. Meet me by the fountain at the end of school."

He sighed theatrically. "Keeping me in suspense, I see."

"Anticipation makes it better," she insisted.

"Fine, I'll be there."

"Perfect," she said, her eyes gleaming. "Don't

forget—fountain, after school. And Noah?"

"Yes?"

"Don't disappear on me," she said pointedly.

He smiled softly. "I won't."

They parted ways as the next bell rang. Noah headed to his Creative Writing class, his mind swirling with possibilities. What could Riley have in store? Whatever it was, he found himself looking forward to it.

Settling into his seat, Noah pulled out his notebook as Mrs. Evans began discussing *The Odyssey*. Her animated voice carried through the classroom as she outlined Odysseus's long journey home and the trials he faced along the way.

"Noah," the teacher called, breaking into his wandering thoughts. "Can you tell us how Odysseus's journey reflects the hero's quest archetype?"

He blinked, scrambling to organize what little he remembered from the book. "Um, well," he began, buying himself a moment. "Odysseus has to overcome a bunch of obstacles—like, uh, the Cyclops and the Sirens—and each one tests a different part of him. His strength, his loyalty, his intelligence. It's through those challenges that he becomes a better leader, and, I guess, a better person."

Mrs. Evans smiled approvingly. "Exactly, Noah. The trials Odysseus faces reveal not only his flaws but also his capacity for growth and resilience. Through adversity, we often find our truest selves."

Her words lingered as Noah jotted down a few notes. For a moment, he stared at the page, the lines of his handwriting blurring. Something about Odysseus's journey stuck with him.

Maybe life was just a series of obstacles, he thought, like one long, unpredictable odyssey. And maybe his own journey was only beginning.

When the final bell of the day rang, Noah felt a mix of nervousness and excitement. After gathering his things, he made his way to the fountain. The water flowed gently, the sound soothing amidst the background chatter of students heading home.

Riley was already there, perched on the edge of the fountain, swinging her legs casually. She looked up as he approached, a broad smile spreading across her face.

"Right on time," she remarked.

"I try," he replied.

She hopped down, her eyes dancing. "Ready for your next adventure?"

He took a deep breath, nodding. "Lead the way."

The courtyard stretched out before them, dotted with a few trees, their leaves rustling softly in the breeze. A few students lingered on benches or made their way toward the parking lot, the end-of-day rush slowly giving way to a more relaxed atmosphere. Riley led him past the last of the lingering students, toward the same tree from yesterday, its branches stretched wide to create a canopy of dappled sunlight.

Here, they could barely hear the noise of the school behind them, and a calm, almost secluded atmosphere surrounded them. Noah felt an odd comfort in this setting, yet he also felt a certain curiosity as he watched Riley settle against the tree. He leaned against the trunk beside her, shoving his hands into his jacket pockets and waiting, letting the quiet linger a moment before he broke it.

"So… what's on your mind?" he asked.

Riley didn't answer right away, but he could see her expression shift to something more serious, her usual smile replaced by a look of intensity. She bit her lower lip, as if weighing her words. Whatever she was about to say felt big, and he found himself leaning slightly closer without even realizing it.

"Okay, so here's the thing," she began. She met his eyes, and her intense expression made Noah feel like the rest of the world had faded away, leaving only the two of them. "There's this party tomorrow night," she announced, watching his reaction closely. "It's supposed to be the party of the year. Everyone who's anyone is going to be there."

Noah frowned, already feeling a familiar knot of apprehension tighten in his stomach. Parties had never been his thing. Just thinking about it made him anxious. "A party?" he repeated, trying to keep his tone neutral. "I'm not the party type."

Riley held up a hand, stopping him before he could retreat any further. "I know, I know," she said. "But hear me out." Her voice had an urgency to it that caught him off guard. "This isn't just any party. It's going to be epic—music, games, dancing. It'll be like stepping into one of those movies you love so much."

Noah gave her a look. "Somehow, I doubt that," he said, though part of him couldn't help but be intrigued. The idea of a John Hughes movie in real life almost sounded like fun, but he pushed the thought aside, not quite ready to let himself be convinced.

Riley leaned closer. "Noah, this could be amazing," she said softly. "Think about it—just for one night, you could let loose and have some fun. No worries, no hiding. Just… living in the present."

He sighed, glancing away as he tried to take in her words. Letting loose wasn't really his style. He preferred his quiet, predictable life. The idea of immersing himself in something as chaotic as a high school party felt daunting.

"I don't know, Riley," he said. "It's just not me. I'd probably end up standing in a corner, counting seconds until I could leave."

Riley tilted her head, a soft smile playing on her lips. "Not if I'm there with you," she said, her voice gentle but insistent.

Noah looked at her, a little surprised by her response. "You'd stick by me the whole time?" he asked, unable to hide the vulnerability in his voice.

"Of course," Riley affirmed without hesitation. "We're a team, aren't we?"

He considered her words, the knot of anxiety in his chest loosening ever so slightly. The thought of going to a party still filled him with dread, but the idea of experiencing it with Riley—of having her by his side—made it seem a little less terrifying. He glanced back at her as he let the idea sink in.

"But… why is this so important to you?" he asked.

Riley took a deep breath as she thought over her answer. "Because I think it's time you stepped out of your comfort zone. I see so much potential in you, Noah. You're creative, thoughtful… there's a whole other side of you that the world deserves to see."

A warm flush rose to Noah's cheeks, and he found himself looking down to avoid her gaze. "I don't know about that," he mumbled.

Riley reached out, placing a hand on his arm. "Trust me," she said softly, her eyes locked onto his. "This could be your chance to be the hero of your own story."

He let out a small laugh, a bit of the tension in his shoulders easing. "You make it sound so dramatic."

She grinned, her playful demeanor returning. "Well, life should be a little dramatic, don't you think?"

Noah hesitated, but felt a sense of curiosity, too. He didn't really like it, but something about Riley's belief in him made him want to try. "I just don't want to feel out of place," he admitted quietly.

"You won't," Riley assured him. "Not with me there. Besides, I happen to think you'll have a great time."

He looked into her eyes, searching for any hint of insincerity, but he found none. Her confidence was contagious, and for once, Noah allowed himself to consider the possibility that she might be right.

"Okay," he said finally, a tentative smile forming. "I'll go."

Riley's face lit up with excitement, her smile so wide that it was impossible not to feel a bit of her enthusiasm. "Yes! I knew you would!" she exclaimed, clapping her hands. "This is going to be so much fun!"

Noah chuckled, shaking his head. "I hope you're right."

"Oh, I am," she replied confidently. "First things first, we'll need to find you the perfect outfit."

He glanced down at his clothes. "What's wrong with my clothes?"

She laughed. "Nothing's wrong with it, but for a party like this, we need to amp it up. Think more... rock star."

Noah raised an eyebrow, his skepticism creeping back. "You're serious?"

"Dead serious," she affirmed with a grin. "Trust me, I've got some ideas."

"I guess I'm in your hands, then."

She beamed. "You won't regret it, I promise."

The breeze picked up, rustling the leaves above them. "So... where is this party anyway?" he asked.

"At Jake's place. His parents are out of town, and he's turning the entire house into a club."

"Jake? As in, Jake Thompson? Quarterback Jake Thompson?" Noah's apprehension returned, thoughts of the popular crowd intimidating him all over again.

Riley waved it off. "Don't worry about him. He's actually pretty chill."

Noah wasn't entirely convinced but decided to let it slide. "If you say so."

She checked her watch. "I should probably get going before my mom wonders where I am."

"Yeah, me too," Noah agreed.

They stood up and began walking toward the parking lot, the late afternoon sun casting long shadows. Riley turned to face him. "Thanks for trusting me," she said quietly.

Noah smiled, warmth blooming in his chest. "Thanks for giving me a reason to."

She gave him a quick hug. "See you tomorrow, Noah."

"See you," he replied as she pulled away.

Noah watched her for a moment before turning to begin his walk home. As he made his way down the familiar streets, his mind buzzed. The idea of attending the party was both thrilling and terrifying. But maybe Riley was right. Maybe it was time to embrace new experiences—even if it was just for one night.

He slipped his headphones over his ears, scrolling until he found his favorite playlist: a mix of synth-pop, rock anthems, and upbeat dance tracks that always seemed to lift his mood. As the familiar opening riff of "Don't Stop Believin'" by Journey filled his ears, he let himself picture the party in vivid detail. He could almost see himself and Riley there, blending into the music and movement, her laughter ringing out over the beat.

He imagined her grabbing his hand and pulling him onto the dance floor, surrounded by people. For the first time, he let himself think that maybe it wouldn't be so bad. Maybe, with Riley's help, he'd even have fun.

CHAPTER FIVE

aturday morning dawned with a gentle glow. The soft rays painted golden patterns on the walls, gradually nudging Noah awake. He lay there for a moment, listening to the distant chirping of birds. The usual stillness of his room was tinged with a buzzing anticipation that made his heart beat a little faster.

Pushing the covers aside, Noah swung his legs over the edge of the bed and sat up. His eyes fell on his denim jacket draped over the back of his chair—a reminder of Riley's suggestion to "amp up" his usual style.

Noah padded across the room to his bathroom, rubbing the last bit of sleep from his eyes. He cranked on the shower, and as the water heated up, he took a moment to study his reflection in the mirror, giving himself an encouraging nod before stepping in.

The warm water hit his shoulders, washing away any lingering grogginess. He found himself humming a tune, his voice bouncing off the shower tiles as he sang a few lines from "Livin' on a Prayer". With the steam swirling around him, he even threw in a few dramatic gestures, as if he were performing for an imaginary crowd. For a moment, he felt that carefree energy Riley was always trying to bring out in him. He laughed to himself, shaking his head at his own antics.

Once he was out and dried off, he ran a comb through his hair, attempting a casual-but-styled look that didn't quite end up as planned. Shrugging, he threw on some deodorant, brushed his teeth, and returned to his room feeling more awake.

He rummaged through his closet, pulling out a shirt he hadn't worn in ages. He swapped his usual jeans for a pair of black ones, giving himself a once-over in the mirror.

"Not exactly rock star material," he muttered.

Sliding on his denim jacket, he felt a small surge of excitement. Maybe today would be different. He took one last look in the mirror. With a steadying breath, he headed out the door, his heart thumping with the possibilities of the day ahead.

In the kitchen, his mom stood at the sink, humming softly along to a tune playing on the radio—a classic ballad that he vaguely recognized.

She turned as he entered, her eyes lighting up. "Well, look who's up and about," she teased, drying her hands on a dish towel. "Good morning, sleepyhead."

"Morning, Mom," he replied, grabbing an apple from the fruit bowl on the counter.

"Plans for today?" his mom asked, leaning casually against the counter with a curious tilt of her head, her eyes studying him with gentle interest.

"Actually, yes," he replied, rubbing the back of his neck—a nervous habit he'd had for as long as he could remember. "Thought I'd go out for a bit." He tried to keep his tone casual, but he knew she could see through him. Going out wasn't exactly his usual Saturday plan.

She raised an eyebrow, a playful smile tugging at her lips. "Oh? Anywhere special?"

He shrugged, aiming for nonchalance. "Just around town. Maybe meet up with a friend." The words felt almost foreign, as if they belonged to someone else. But they sounded good—right, even. Just the thought of having plans felt like a step forward.

Her smile widened, a genuine warmth lighting up her eyes. "That sounds fun," she said, and reached out and placed a hand on his shoulder. "Enjoy yourself, alright? Have fun. You deserve it."

"I will," he promised. Her encouragement felt like a quiet push forward. She always seemed to know exactly what he needed to hear.

As he turned to leave, she called after him. "Oh, and Noah?"

He paused in the doorway, looking back over his shoulder. "Yeah?"

She gave him a small, encouraging nod. "I'm proud of you."

He felt a flicker of warmth in his chest, filling him with a quiet confidence. "Thanks, Mom," he said.

With one last smile, he stepped out of the house, letting the door close gently behind him. The sky was a clear expanse of blue, the sun shining brightly. He closed his eyes for a moment, letting the fresh air fill his lungs, calming his jittery nerves.

He walked over to the side of the house where his bike was propped against the wall. It was a bit old, with chipped paint and a slight squeak in the pedals, but it had been reliable for years.

The neighborhood was peaceful at this time of morning. A few cars rolled by, their engines blending with birdsong. And the morning air was crisp, carrying the faint scent of fresh-cut grass. He pedaled steadily, the quiet rhythm of the wheels turning and the gentle breeze against his face.

After a few more turns and several blocks, the city park came into view at the end of the street, stretching out wide and green, a lively scene even from a distance. The energy of the place was undeniable—children playing on the swings, joggers passing by, friends laughing together on picnic blankets.

Finally, he reached the park entrance, pulling to a stop as he took it all in. He swung his leg off the bike and wheeled it over to a rack, securing it. He scanned the area and the clusters of people until he spotted her sitting on a bench. She was watching him, a bright smile lighting up her face.

"You made it!" Riley called out, scooting over to make room for him.

"Of course I did," he replied, smiling as he sat down beside her.

Riley stretched out her legs and leaned back, looking out over the park. "Isn't it great here?" she said, gesturing toward the groups scattered around the park. "All that energy… people just living their lives."

He nodded, feeling at ease in her presence. "It is," he admitted, surprised by how different everything seemed with her beside him.

Riley pointed at a group of kids playing Frisbee nearby, their laughter and carefree banter drifting over to them. "You ever play Frisbee?"

Noah shook his head, smiling faintly. "Sports aren't really my thing. Besides, I'm a stranger."

Riley rolled her eyes, undeterred. "So what? They're just out here having fun. You could join in for five minutes, no big deal." She nudged him again. "Come on, live a little."

He looked over at the group, watching them for a moment, then back at Riley. She gave him an encouraging smile, and before he could talk himself out of it, he nodded. "Alright... but just for a bit."

Riley's face lit up, and she jumped to her feet, tugging him up with her. As they made their way over, one of the players—a boy around twelve with tousled brown hair—missed a catch, sending the Frisbee skidding to a stop a few feet in front of Noah.

Taking it as a sign, Noah bent down to pick it up, giving the boy a friendly smile. "Lose something?"

The boy jogged over, grinning sheepishly. "Yeah, thanks! That was all me."

"No worries," Noah replied, handing it over, and after a quick glance at Riley, he added, "Mind if I join for a bit?"

The boy's face brightened. "Sure! We could use another player. I'm Max."

Noah introduced himself as Riley took a seat back on the bench, and was quickly pulled into the rhythm of their game. At first, he felt a bit self-conscious, unsure if he'd keep up, but the group was friendly and easygoing, cheering him on with every throw and catch. The Frisbee flew back and forth, and Noah found himself diving for it, laughing when he missed, and high-fiving the others when they made a good grab.

A few minutes into the game, Max called out, "Heads up, Noah!" and sent the Frisbee sailing his way. Noah tracked it carefully, stretching his arms just in time to make the catch. Cheers erupted from the group, and he couldn't help but smile as he tossed it back.

"Nice throw, Noah!" Max shouted after him as the Frisbee soared across the field.

"Thanks!" he called back, feeling a genuine smile spread across his face. He glanced over at the bench and caught Riley's eye; she gave him an enthusiastic thumbs-up. He felt a spark of confidence he hadn't felt in a long time, enjoying the easy camaraderie of the game.

After several rounds, the game began to wind down, and some of the kids' parents started gathering near the picnic tables. One mom called over, "Max! Time to eat!"

Max jogged over, grabbing his water bottle and giving a wave. "I gotta go," he said, smiling at Noah. "Thanks for playing with us! You're really good."

"Sure," Noah replied, waving back. "Thanks for letting me join in."

Max gave a quick nod and ran off to join his family. Noah watched the kids head to the picnic tables, feeling a lightness he hadn't felt in ages. He walked back to the bench where Riley sat, still a bit breathless, but exhilarated.

She grinned at him as he sat down, her eyes filled with pride. "You did great out there."

He leaned back, still catching his breath, and let out a long, contented sigh. "I don't usually do things like that," he admitted, glancing at her with a slight smile.

Riley nudged his shoulder. "Maybe that's why you should. You're a natural."

Noah smiled, feeling a warmth in his chest. "Yeah... maybe you're right."

Riley stood up, stretching as she looked around the park with an eager glint in her eye. "And that was just the start. There's so much more to do today," she said, offering her hand with a playful smile. "Come on, let's keep the adventure going."

He took her hand, standing up beside her. "Alright, what's next?"

Riley beamed, looping her arm through his as they started back toward the bike rack. "How about the arcade?" she suggested. "It's been ages since I've been there."

He nodded to himself. "Arcade it is."

They set off toward the older part of town, riding side by side down the quiet streets. Riley chatted excitedly, pointing out little details along the way—the way a particular house looked like it belonged in a storybook or how the scent from a nearby bakery reminded her of her grandmother's cinnamon rolls.

The streets soon became narrower, lined with mom-and-pop shops displaying everything from antiques to handmade crafts. "I love this part of town," Riley said, her voice laced with nostalgia. "It feels like stepping back in time, you know?"

Noah nodded. "It's got a certain charm. You don't see many places like this anymore."

They eventually arrived at the arcade—a small, unassuming building with a neon sign that flickered "Game Zone." Riley's eyes lit up as she spotted it. "This place is a gem! I used to come here all the time. Come on!"

Inside, they were met with a symphony of electronic sounds. Riley practically dragged him down the aisles, her enthusiasm infectious as she pointed out her favorite games from childhood.

"Look! They have *Street Fighter II*," Riley said, nudging him with her elbow. "Think you've got some moves?"

Noah fished a coin from his pocket. "Only one way to find out."

He slid the coin into the slot, and the machine hummed to life, its screen flickering as the game's title flashed in bold letters. Familiar faces appeared on the character selection screen, and with a surge of excitement, Noah hovered over Ryu before hitting the button to confirm.

"Ryu? Really?" Riley teased, leaning against the side of the machine with her arms crossed. "Not exactly a risk-taker, are you?"

He smirked, adjusting his grip on the joystick. "Sometimes, classics are classics for a reason."

The match started, pitting Ryu against Ken in the iconic stage set against a backdrop of waterfalls and temples. Noah's focus sharpened as he moved the joystick, landing quick punches and blocking Ken's attacks.

"Hadouken!" Noah called out as he executed Ryu's

signature fireball move, the blue energy blast connecting with Ken mid-jump.

"Oh, okay!" Riley said, clapping lightly. "I see you know your stuff."

Ken retaliated with a Shoryuken, but Noah dodged, weaving Ryu into a spinning kick that brought Ken's health bar down to a sliver. Riley cheered as Noah landed the final blow with a perfectly timed uppercut, the screen flashing "K.O."

"Not bad, Harper," she teased as he scored the victory. "Guess you haven't lost your touch."

He shot her a playful look, raising an eyebrow. "Care to try and beat my score?"

"Oh, I don't think so," she laughed, hands held up in surrender. "I'd just embarrass myself. Besides, watching you show off is way more entertaining."

They wandered around the arcade, the air alive with a mix of electronic beeps, whirs, and the occasional cheer from other players. The soft glow of lights reflected off the shiny linoleum floor, casting streaks of colors as they weaved between rows of machines.

Riley stopped in front of *Ms. Pac-Man*, the screen flickering with the familiar maze and bright ghosts zipping around. "Alright, let's see if I've still got it," she said, cracking her knuckles theatrically before gripping the joystick.

Noah leaned against the side of the cabinet, arms crossed, watching as Riley expertly navigated the maze, gobbling dots and power pellets. "You're weirdly good at this," he remarked, raising an eyebrow as she narrowly dodged Blinky and Pinky.

She smirked, keeping her eyes glued to the screen. "I used to crush this game at the pizza place by my house. Free slice if you beat the high score."

"That explains a lot," Noah said, grinning as she cleared the board and advanced to the next level, the familiar jingle playing through the tinny speakers.

They moved on when the game ended, stopping at *Tron*, where Noah took the reins. The joystick felt stiff in his hand, but the game's vibrant blue grid and flashing discs instantly transported him back. "This game is so unfair," he muttered as his digital avatar disintegrated into pixels for the third time.

"Maybe it's the player, not the game," Riley teased.

"Oh, you think you can do better?" Noah said, gesturing toward the machine.

"Pass," Riley said, holding up her hands. "I'll stick to games that don't make me want to throw things."

Further down the aisle, the claw machine caught their eye. Its bright pink sign boasted *"Win Big!"* over a bed of stuffed animals.

"Piece of cake," Noah said, eyes narrowing in concentration. He slid a few coins into the slot, gripping the joystick and maneuvered the claw above a plush dinosaur.

The claw descended, grabbing the dinosaur by the tail before loosening its grip and letting it drop back into the pile at the last second. "No!" Noah groaned, throwing his head back dramatically.

Riley clapped her hands, laughing. "So close! Maybe you'll get it next time, champ."

Noah shook his head, feigning disappointment.

"These things are rigged. I could've landed that."

"Sure, blame the machine," Riley said with a grin, nudging him toward the next row of games.

The arcade buzzed with nostalgia, from the faint sound of *Galaga* in the background to the smell of popcorn and faintly burnt circuits. Noah couldn't help but feel a strange comfort in the timeless energy of the place, like they'd stepped into a pocket of the past where nothing else mattered except high scores and glowing screens.

Eventually, they came across a small crowd gathered around a *Dance Dance Revolution* machine. The flashing lights and pounding bass filled the corner of the arcade, drawing their attention immediately. Riley's eyes sparkled as she took in the energetic scene, then turned to Noah with a wide grin.

"Oh, we have to try this," she said, nudging him with an almost mischievous look.

Noah raised an eyebrow, taking a small step back. "I don't think so," he replied, shaking his head. "I'll make a fool of myself."

"Exactly," she countered, her grin widening as she grabbed his hand, pulling him toward the machine before he could protest. "That's the fun part! Besides, I promise I'll go easy on you."

He hesitated, glancing around at the onlookers who cheered on the current players. His heart raced, and he felt the familiar tug of self-doubt, the anxiety. But Riley's hand in his felt steady, grounding him, and her enthusiasm was contagious.

"Alright," he sighed. "But if I fall on my face, you're

taking the blame."

She laughed, squeezing his hand reassuringly. "Deal. Just follow the arrows and have fun. Trust me."

As they stepped up to the machine, the crowd around them clapped in encouragement. The first notes of a fast-paced song blasted through the speakers, and the arrows started lighting up on the screen in rapid succession. He focused on the beat, trying to follow the movements, though his steps were awkward.

Riley moved beside him with surprising ease, her feet light and quick, perfectly timed with the rhythm. She laughed, calling out little instructions to him between steps, her voice encouraging. "Just let go and move with the beat, Noah! You've got this!"

He looked over at her, and something about the way she danced so freely, without a care for how she looked, inspired him. A burst of laughter escaped him as he finally gave in, letting his steps follow the beat, even if they were clumsy. He stumbled, missed arrows, but none of it seemed to matter. Every mistake was met with her laughter, her joy only growing each time he loosened up a little more.

The song ended, and he turned to her, breathless and grinning. "I can't believe I just did that," he said, still smiling as the machine tallied the score. His was laughably low.

Riley shrugged, nudging him with her shoulder. "Not bad for a first try, Harper," she teased, her tone light but filled with genuine pride.

He shook his head a warmth spread through him that had nothing to do with the dance. "Yeah," he said, still catching his breath. The small crowd around them clapped, and Noah felt an unexpected thrill at the applause—even if it was just a game, it was a rush he hadn't felt before.

Riley gave him a proud grin, nudging his shoulder playfully. "See? You survived."

He laughed, still processing the excitement that pulsed through him. "'Survived' is about right."

Riley tilted her head, watching him with a smile. "You look different, you know," she said, her voice quieter, almost thoughtful. "Like... you're enjoying yourself."

He met her gaze. "Maybe I am," he replied, almost as if he was admitting it to himself. "This day, it's been—" He paused, searching for the right words. "It's like a different world in here. Kind of fun, actually."

Riley beamed, clearly pleased with his response. "Exactly. There's a whole lot out there just waiting for you, Noah. And you've barely scratched the surface." She glanced back at the *Dance Dance Revolution* machine, her eyes shining with that familiar spark of challenge. "Want to go again? Maybe you'll beat me this time."

He smirked, feeling a new surge of confidence. "Alright, one more round."

They stepped back onto the machine, and this time Noah didn't hold back. The beat kicked in, and he followed the arrows, laughing every time he stumbled. He let himself fall deeper into the moment, his movements more relaxed and confident.

As they finally stepped off, still catching their breath,

Riley's eyes caught on something just a few feet away. She gasped, grabbing Noah's arm. "No way! A photo booth!"

Noah followed her gaze to the corner where the vintage booth stood, its metallic exterior gleaming faintly under the arcade's neon glow. "You mean one of those old-school ones?" he asked, tilting his head.

"Yes!" she said, already tugging him toward it. "Come on, it'll be fun!"

Before he could protest, she shoved a handful of coins into the machine and pulled back the curtain. "Get in!" she urged, practically pushing him inside.

The booth was snug, the seats covered in cracked vinyl. Riley sat beside him, leaning close to fit them both in the frame. "Okay," she said, her hand hovering over the button. "First one: serious faces."

The camera flashed, capturing their awkwardly stoic expressions.

"Alright, now… silly!" Riley shouted, crossing her eyes while throwing up peace signs. Noah hesitated for a second before sticking his tongue out.

The next flash went off, and Riley laughed. "Last one: surprise me."

Noah's lips quirked into a sly grin as an idea struck him. Without warning, he reached up and tousled Riley's hair, catching her mid-protest as the final flash went off.

When the strip of photos printed, Riley grabbed it first, her eyes widening as she got to the last frame. "Seriously?" she exclaimed, holding it up to him. Her hair was a mess, her expression caught somewhere between surprise and mock indignation.

"You said *surprise*." He smirked.

"These are perfect," Riley said, still giggling. "You're keeping these, by the way."

"Wait, why me?" Noah protested.

"Because you need reminders of how fun you are," she said simply, tucking the strip into his jacket pocket before he could argue. "Now, onward! I think we've officially conquered this arcade," she said.

"Alright," he said, breaking into a smile. "What's next?"

"How about the record store?" she suggested.

"Lead the way," he replied with a grin.

CHAPTER SIX

They headed to "Retro Beats," a small shop nestled between a nail salon and a bookstore. The sign above the door was a bit worn, its paint chipped in places, but Riley gave it an affectionate pat as they entered.

Inside, they were greeted by rows of vinyl records, CDs, and even a few old cassettes, filling the air with the faint scent of aged paper and something subtly sweet—maybe a candle burning somewhere. The place had a lived-in feeling, like it was a part of history itself, frozen in time but still pulsing with life.

"Oh, this place has so much character," Riley sighed, her voice soft with admiration as she wandered down the aisles. She ran her fingers gently over the album covers like they were delicate artifacts. Sunlight streamed in from the shop's front windows, casting a warm glow over the rows of vinyl, their unique designs and textures hinting at different eras.

"Check this out," Noah said, pausing in front of a display case near the entrance. Inside were rare editions—albums with handwritten notes, limited pressings, and even a framed *Abbey Road* signed by Paul McCartney.

"Imagine owning that," Riley said, her eyes widening as she pointed to the framed record. "You could hang it on your wall and just stare at it all day."

"I think if I owned it, I'd be too scared to touch it," Noah admitted. "What if it fell or got scratched? That's like destroying history."

Riley smirked, nudging him. "You're such a careful soul, Harper. Sometimes you've just got to live a little."

Noah laughed softly, shaking his head as they moved deeper into the shop, their footsteps muffled by a faded carpet runner that stretched between the aisles. The faint sound of David Bowie hummed in the background.

Riley picked up an old Fleetwood Mac album. "Okay, you can't tell me *Rumours* isn't one of the greatest albums of all time," she said, holding it up triumphantly.

Noah smirked. "Bold claim. I mean, it's good, but…"

"But what?" Riley interrupted, narrowing her eyes. "Don't even say it's overrated. I will walk out right now."

"Relax, it's a classic," Noah said, raising his hands defensively. "I was going to say it's the kind of album you can listen to front to back without skipping anything. That's rare."

"Exactly," Riley said, satisfied. "You do have taste."

As they reached a particularly narrow aisle, Noah shifted to let Riley squeeze past him. And just as Noah turned to follow, his foot caught the edge of a low rack filled with bargain-bin records.

It happened fast. One second he was upright, the next he stumbled forward, nearly toppling into a nearby shelf. The rack rattled loudly as a few records slid to the floor in dramatic, clattering fashion.

Riley whipped around, wide-eyed. "Oh my gosh, are you okay?"

Noah quickly righted himself, his face burning as he crouched down to pick up the scattered records. "Yeah, yeah, I'm fine. Just, uh… testing the durability of the inventory."

Riley bit her lip, trying—and failing—to hide a grin. "You're smooth, Harper. Really. Like a bull in a record shop."

"Glad my embarrassment is so entertaining for you," he muttered, stacking the records back in the bin. "I'm sure this will go down in the shop's history as the Great Vinyl Rack Incident of 2025."

The shopkeeper appeared from behind a corner, his gray eyebrows raised. "Everything alright over here?"

"Yep, all good," Noah said quickly. "No records were harmed in the making of this disaster."

The shopkeeper chuckled. "Happens more often than you'd think. Those bins are tricky. Watch your step, young man."

Riley, still smirking, patted Noah on the shoulder. "You're making quite an impression."

"Glad I could contribute," he said with a reluctant grin.

They moved on, Riley pausing in front of a shelf marked "Psychedelic Rock." She pulled out a record with a bold, swirling design of neon oranges, purples, and greens that seemed to pulse under the light. Across the top, the title *Electric Ladyland* by The Jimi Hendrix Experience was emblazoned in flowing script.

Grinning, she held it up to Noah. "What do you think? A little Hendrix to expand your horizons?"

Noah chuckled, shaking his head. "Maybe if I were

trying to time travel back to Woodstock," he teased.

Riley rolled her eyes playfully. "Okay, Mr. Music Critic. What's your pick, then?"

He scanned the shelves, his eyes lingering over familiar names and vibrant covers until he reached the "Alternative/Indie" section. Suddenly, he spotted a name he recognized. "The Smiths," he murmured, pulling out an album with a simple, sepia-toned cover featuring a man gazing thoughtfully off to the side.

Riley peered over his shoulder. "The Smiths? I didn't know you were into them."

He shrugged. "I'm not—well, not really. My cousin used to play them all the time when we'd hang out. This one was his favorite."

Before Riley could reply, a voice chimed in from behind them. "Good choice."

They turned to find the shopkeeper standing beside them with a warm smile. "That one's a classic," he said, nodding at the album in Noah's hand. "There's something special about The Smiths. It's raw, honest—music that sticks with you."

Noah turned the album over in his hands, feeling an inexplicable connection to it. "Do you have a favorite track from this one?"

The man's face brightened as he thought. "Oh, that's a tough one," he said, adjusting his glasses thoughtfully. "But I'd say 'There Is a Light That Never Goes Out' gets me every time. It's haunting, in the best way."

Noah glanced down at the album again, feeling like the songs inside might hold some hidden message meant for him. "I'll take it," he said, a hint of excitement in his voice.

The shopkeeper nodded approvingly. "Good choice, my friend. There's just something about vinyl—it has a soul, you know? You can feel the music in a way you just can't with digital."

Riley's eyes lit up as she nodded in agreement, clearly captivated by the shopkeeper's passion. "I love that. It's like a whole experience."

"Every album has a story just waiting to be told," the man continued with a grin, gesturing to the shelves around them.

They walked together to the counter, where the shopkeeper carefully wrapped the record in a paper bag decorated with musical notes. As he handed it over, he offered a final, encouraging smile. "Enjoy the music, and don't be a stranger. The best albums find their way into your life when you least expect it."

"Thank you," Noah said, returning the smile, feeling a deeper appreciation for this hidden gem of a shop.

Riley gave the shopkeeper a quick wave, and they headed out the door, stepping back onto the sunlit sidewalk.

With the record tucked safely in his arms, Noah felt a strange connection to something bigger, something timeless. Riley linked her arm through his, her eyes shining with excitement.

"So, what's next on the adventure list, Mr. Indie Vinyl Collector?"

He looked at his watch, realizing it was getting late. "Maybe some food?"

Riley grinned. "Perfect. And while we eat, I'll

educate you on why Hendrix is a must-have for your collection. Prepare yourself."

Noah laughed, shaking his head as they strolled down the sidewalk. They walked to an old-fashioned diner at the edge of town, a place Noah remembered from his childhood. The "Silver Spoon" had a retro vibe, with chrome accents, checkered floors, and red vinyl booths. The bell above the door chimed as they entered, the scent of frying bacon and fresh coffee welcoming them in.

Riley slid into a booth by the window, smoothing the edges of her jacket. Noah dropped into the seat across from her and leaned his elbows lightly on the table.

"This is perfect," Riley said, glancing out the window. "A good view and just the right amount of retro charm. Ten out of ten diner vibes."

Noah chuckled, nodding as he took in the space. The chrome accents, faint hum of chatter, and distant clinking of dishes gave the place a timeless energy. "Yeah, it's got character," he said, glancing down at the laminated menu on the table.

The waitress appeared, a friendly woman with a well-worn notepad in hand. "What can I get for you?" she asked.

Noah picked up the menu, his eyes scanning it briefly before he closed it with a decisive nod. "I'll have a chocolate milkshake".

"Really? Going all out, aren't we?" Riley joked, her eyes sparkling with amusement.

He feigned seriousness, meeting her gaze with a mock-stern expression. "Hey, it's a special day. I deserve it."

Riley laughed, rolling her eyes. "Alright, but you'd better let me have a sip."

Noah smirked and leaned forward. "You want anything?"

Riley shook her head. "Nah, I'll just help with whatever you get."

He shrugged and looked back at the waitress. "We'd add a side of fries with the milkshake."

The waitress nodded, giving him a funny look as she turned and headed toward the kitchen.

Riley tilted her head. "Fries and a milkshake? You're really going for it."

"Classic combo," Noah said with a smirk. "And now you don't have to steal too much of my milkshake."

"No promises," Riley teased, leaning back in her seat, clearly enjoying herself.

She leaned forward, her elbow resting on the table as she examined the small jukebox. "Okay, real question— do you think this actually works, or is it just here for the aesthetic?"

Noah craned his neck to get a better look. The dusty metal casing and scuffed buttons didn't inspire much confidence. "I'm guessing it's about a fifty-fifty shot. But there's only one way to find out."

Riley pulled a quarter from her pocket and slid it into the slot. With a small click, the machine hummed faintly to life, its dim light flickering. She scanned the list of song titles printed on faded paper strips behind the glass, her finger hovering over a row.

"Oh my gosh," she said, her eyes lighting up. "They have 'Earth Angel'. This is such a *Back to the Future* moment. You want me to play it?"

"Sure," Noah said with a shrug. "But only if you're prepared to start slow dancing in the middle of the diner."

She laughed, pressing the button for the song. "You say that like it's a dare."

As the music crackled through the small speakers, the soft, nostalgic tune filled the air, blending perfectly with the retro charm of the diner. Riley swayed slightly in her seat, tapping her fingers against the table in time with the music.

"You know," she said, glancing at him, "this place kind of makes you want to live in the 50's. Like, wouldn't it be cool to be here back when this was new? You'd probably be sitting here in a leather jacket, and a white t-shirt, trying to act cool."

Noah laughed, shaking his head. "Me? Cool? I'd be George McFly."

"Please, you'd totally be the rebel who rolls up on a motorcycle," she teased, pretending to rev invisible handlebars. "You've got that mysterious vibe."

Noah snorted. "Yeah, because nothing says 'mysterious' like tripping over a rack at a record store."

Riley grinned. "Alright, maybe you'd be the guy fixing the jukebox instead. Quiet, brooding, but secretly the hero."

Before he could respond, the waitress arrived with a tall glass topped with whipped cream and a cherry. She set it down with a smile. "Here you go—one chocolate milkshake. And a plate of fries."

Noah grinned, eyeing the milkshake as if it were a trophy. He took the first sip, the rich, creamy taste making him close his eyes in appreciation.

"Good?" Riley asked, resting her chin in her hand, watching him with an amused smile.

"Perfect," Noah said, sliding the glass toward her. "Alright, go ahead. You said you wanted a sip."

She took the straw and leaned forward, sipping delicately before sitting back with a nod. "Okay, that's pretty good. You might be onto something."

"See? I'm full of great ideas," Noah teased, nudging the glass back toward himself.

Riley smirked. "Oh, really? So, if you're such a genius, what's the best way to skip school without getting caught?"

Noah blinked, caught off guard by the question. "Wait—why are we skipping school?"

"Why not?" Riley leaned back in the booth, crossing her arms with a grin. "Life's short, Harper. You gotta dance in the daylight—break the rules and just live a little."

Noah raised an eyebrow, leaning forward. "Alright, fine. Step one: Find a good excuse. Like, you're sick. But you've got to sell it—get the cough just right, maybe splash some water on your face to look sweaty."

Riley nodded, pretending to take notes. "Sick day strategy. Classic. What's step two?"

"Step two…" Noah paused, thinking. "You've got to make it worth it. If you're just gonna sit at home, what's the point? You need an epic plan—like sneaking into a movie, or going to… I don't know, a water park."

"A water park?" Riley laughed. "You're skipping school to ride a lazy river?"

"Not just the lazy river. The slides, too," Noah shot back. "You've got to go big."

Riley shook her head, still laughing. "Alright, Harper, let's say you pull this off. What's step three?"

"Step three: Cover your tracks. Leave no evidence. That means no selfies, no social media, and definitely no telling anyone who'll rat you out."

"Impressive," Riley said, giving him an exaggerated slow clap. "You've clearly thought this through."

"Hey, you asked," Noah replied with a shrug, sipping his milkshake.

Riley leaned forward, her eyes sparkling with mischief. "So, when are we putting this master plan into action?"

"Wait, we're actually doing this?"

"Why not?" Riley said with a grin. "Come on, Noah. You've got the perfect plan. Let's see if it works."

Noah laughed, shaking his head. "You're trouble, you know that?"

"Yeah," Riley said, grabbing a fry from the plate. "But I'm fun."

They took turns, laughing as they swapped stories, each sharing small details about their lives. Riley told him about the time she and her sister decided to make milkshakes after watching a cooking channel on TV. "We didn't measure anything," she said. "We just dumped ice cream, milk, and chocolate syrup into the blender like we'd done it a hundred times. But when we turned it on, we forgot to put on the lid, and—boom! Ice cream everywhere. Ceiling, cabinets, even in the toaster."

Noah burst out laughing. "Please tell me you cleaned

it up before your parents saw it."

"Oh, we tried," Riley said, rolling her eyes. "But Mom walked in halfway through. She took one look at the kitchen and just started laughing. We spent the next hour scrubbing everything."

Noah shook his head, still chuckling. "Remind me to never let you near a blender."

"Fair warning," Riley said with a smile.

Noah shared a memory from when he was ten and decided to build a treehouse with a couple of friends. "We just found some old wood in my neighbor's shed and a bucket of nails," he said. "Figured, how hard could it be?"

"And?" Riley asked, leaning forward, her eyes sparkling with curiosity.

"It was a disaster," he admitted, laughing. "We barely got the floorboards nailed down before one of the guys leaned on it to test it out. The whole thing collapsed in, like, two seconds. We all just stood there staring at the mess in this huge pile of broken branches and wood. Pretty sure one of us cried."

Riley gasped, covering her mouth. "Wait, you cried?"

"No, not me," Noah said quickly, holding up his hands. "It was Kevin. He was, like, eight, and he thought he was gonna get grounded for wrecking the backyard."

"Did you guys ever try again?" Riley asked.

"Nope," he said, shaking his head with a grin. "Figured I'd leave construction to the professionals after that. My dad told me it was 'character building'."

They both laughed, leaning back in the booth as the milkshake glass sat nearly empty between them, just a swirl of melted chocolate and whipped cream left at the bottom. Outside, the sun was sinking lower, casting a warm, golden glow through the diner windows. The chrome and red vinyl shimmered in the late sun, making it feel like a scene from a movie.

"Thanks for today," Noah said after a beat. His voice was quiet, like he wasn't sure if he should say it out loud. "I don't think I'd have done half of this without you."

Riley tilted her head and met his eyes. "Anytime. But don't sell yourself short—you did all this, Noah. I just tagged along."

Noah shook his head, fiddling with the edge of a napkin. "No, really. You make things... easier. Like, I don't feel like I have to be on guard all the time. That's rare for me."

Her smile turned more thoughtful, and she leaned forward, resting her chin in her hand. "Why do you think you're always on guard? Like, what are you so worried about?"

He shrugged, avoiding her gaze. "I don't know. Maybe I just got used to it. People can be... pretty ruthless. It's like, if they can find a way to mess with you, they will. So, it's easier to stay invisible, right?"

Riley frowned slightly, her fingers drumming lightly on the table. "Is that why you didn't say anything to Todd yesterday? Because staying quiet felt safer?"

Noah's jaw tightened, his grip on the napkin crumpling slightly. "It's not like I let him mess with me," he said, his voice defensive. "It's just... what's the point? Todd's one of those guys who always wins. Even if you stand up to him, it just makes things worse."

"Does it?" Riley countered gently. "Or is that what you tell yourself so you don't have to deal with conflict?"

Noah looked up, his brows furrowing. "What am I supposed to do, Riley? Yell at him? Punch him? All that does is make me look like the bad guy. People like Todd… they've already won before the fight even starts."

She leaned back, her voice soft. "Noah, you're letting him live rent-free in your head. Every time you stay quiet, he gets to feel bigger, stronger. But you? You get smaller. And the worst part? You're the one shrinking yourself."

He blinked, taken aback by the bluntness of her words. "It's not that simple," he muttered.

"I know it's not," Riley said, her tone gentler now. "But letting someone like Todd define who you are? That's giving him way too much power. You don't have to fight him, but you also don't have to just… let him win. There's a middle ground."

Noah sighed, leaning back in the booth. "What's the middle ground then? Enlighten me, oh Yoda."

Riley smiled faintly. "You start by not believing the crap he says about you. He calls you 'Space Cadet'? Fine. Own it. Turn it into a compliment. Like, yeah, you zone out sometimes—so what? Maybe it's because you're thinking about something bigger than his dumb insults."

Noah let out a dry laugh, shaking his head. "You really think that's gonna stop him?"

"No," Riley admitted. "But it'll stop him from getting to you. And that's the point, right? You can't control what he says, but you can control how much space you let him take up in your life."

He didn't respond right away, her words sinking in as

he stared at the empty glass between them. Finally, he spoke, his voice quiet. "You make it sound easy."

"It's not," Riley said, leaning forward again. "But it gets easier when you stop fighting yourself. Todd's not your biggest enemy, Noah. You are."

That hit harder than he wanted to admit. He stared out the window for a moment. "You've thought about this a lot, haven't you?"

Riley nodded. "Yeah. I decided a long time ago I'd rather be myself than someone I'm not. Because being invisible? That hurts just as much as being judged."

Noah looked at her. "How do you do it, though? Just... not care?"

"I didn't say I don't care," Riley replied. "I care a lot. But I realized I can't change what other people think. The only thing I can change is how much I let it affect me."

Noah nodded slowly, letting her words settle in. There was something about the way she said it—calm, certain—that made it hard to argue.

Riley slid out of the booth, her smile returning. "Something tells me this isn't the last milkshake we'll share."

Noah chuckled, following her toward the door. "I'll hold you to that."

As they stepped outside, the bell jingled behind them, and the cool evening air greeted them. For a moment, they stood in silence, the golden-pink sky stretching above them.

"You know," Riley said, looping her arm through his, "next time Todd says something dumb, you should try calling him out. Just once."

"And say what?" Noah asked, raising an eyebrow.

"Whatever comes to mind," she replied. "You've got a good brain, Harper. Use it. Todd's whole shtick falls apart if people stop laughing at his jokes. Trust me."

They started walking, the diner fading into the distance. Noah felt lighter somehow, as if the weight of the day—the weight of Todd—was a little easier to carry now. Riley had a way of doing that, of making him feel like maybe he didn't have to carry it all alone. For the first time in a long while, the noise in his head was quiet.

Riley pointed to a thrift store down the block. Above the door, a sign read "Second Chances," the letters curled in playful script and dotted with whimsical stars. "Want to go in?"

As they approached Noach glanced at the eclectic display in the window. Vintage clothing, old books, and curious knick-knacks beckoned invitingly. A 70's coat hung on a mannequin next to a stack of dusty photo albums, and beside it, a small ceramic owl perched awkwardly atop a pile of faded comic books.

Noah let out a breath. "I've walked by this place a hundred times. Never thought to go in."

Riley leaned closer, peering through the glass. "Your loss. Places like this are full of treasure. You've just got to be willing to dig a little."

"Treasure, huh?" he said. "You mean like that owl?"

She grinned. "Don't knock it. That owl's got personality."

Noah laughed softly. "Thanks," he said suddenly.

Riley glanced at him. "For what?"

"For just... being you," he said.

She bumped his shoulder playfully. "Anytime, Harper. Now let's find something else to make fun of you for."

CHAPTER SEVEN

Noah squared his shoulders and pushed open the glass door. The moment he stepped inside, he was enveloped by a tapestry of scents—the mustiness of old fabric mingled with the rich aroma of polished wood and a faint hint of patchouli. The air was cool, and the soft, amber lighting created an atmosphere that felt both inviting and timeless, like he'd just walked into another era.

He paused at the entrance. Rows of racks and shelves created a maze of colors and textures. Vintage dresses with intricate lace details hung beside a wall of well-worn leather shoes. Shelves overflowed with an assortment of accessories—hats, scarves, belts, and jewelry—all waiting to be rediscovered and given new life.

"Let's start with something bold," Riley said. She leaned closer, lowering her voice like she was sharing a secret. "Something that makes you feel like the lead in your favorite movie."

Noah raised an eyebrow, the corner of his mouth tugging upward in a reluctant grin. "Alright... bold it is."

As he browsed, he trailed his fingers across the different fabrics. Something began to stir in him—a feeling he couldn't quite pin down. He rounded a corner and stopped. There they were: jackets. Not just any jackets, though. These were bold, unapologetic pieces of art. Bright reds, electric blues, deep greens. Sequins that caught the light, patches that practically screamed for attention, graphic prints that could've walked straight out of an MTV music video from 1985.

One jacket stood out—a vibrant blue letterman with sleeves and a chest covered in patches. Lightning bolts, stars, peace signs. Some of the patches had phrases, ones that seemed to whisper a dare: *Ride the Lightning. Stay Wild.*

Noah reached out and his hand brushed the fabric. It was softer than he'd expected, but solid, like it had weight. The satin lining glided under his fingers, and he could already picture himself wearing this jacket and walking into a room with all eyes on him. Not because he was trying, but because he'd let himself *be seen* for once.

"Try it on, Noah," Riley said. Her voice was light, but there was something knowing in her smile. "Trust me."

He hesitated, glancing at her, then back at the jacket. Taking a deep breath, he shrugged off his denim jacket and slid into the letterman. The weight settled over his shoulders like it had been waiting for him. The fit was perfect—not too tight, not too loose. Just *right.*

Turning toward a mirror, Noah felt a pang of uncertainty. What if it was too much? What if—?

But then his reflection stopped him. The electric blue made his dark hair and eyes stand out in a way that surprised him. His reflection wasn't just familiar—it was magnetic. The patches weren't just decoration. They felt like a preview of someone new, someone braver.

"You look amazing," Riley said.

He tilted his head. "Not bad," he said, though inside, he felt something else entirely. Confidence. Not the kind you fake but the kind that sneaks up on you when you realize you've been standing in your own way. Amazing how a single piece of clothing could do that.

Riley's grin widened. "C'mon. You need the full look."

He followed her deeper into the store. When they reached the graphic tees, he stopped, drawn to the explosion of colors and prints. He thumbed through band logos and sharp geometric designs, pausing when one shirt seemed to leap out at him.

It was black, but streaked with vibrant swaths of electric blue, pink, and yellow. It didn't just match; it felt like it belonged with the letterman jacket... as if the two pieces were meant to find each other.

"This is it," he said, holding up the shirt.

Riley gave an approving nod, and for a moment, Noah let himself feel it—that quiet spark of rightness, of things clicking into place.

Jeans came next. An entire wall of options stretched out before him. Noah's fingers brushed over faded denim, torn knees, and washes that ranged from inky black to a weathered gray. But it was a pair of dark-wash jeans that caught his attention—slim-fit, with just a hint of stretch.

He pulled them from the rack, holding them up to inspect the cut. They were a far cry from the baggy, relaxed pairs that usually dominated his wardrobe. These jeans had a shape, a deliberate fit designed to frame rather than hide. They didn't scream for attention, but they didn't shy away from it, either.

As he draped them over his arm, he could already feel the quiet rebellion in the choice. They weren't flashy like the jacket or chaotic like the tee, but they represented something more personal—a step outside the safe, shapeless styles he always chose. These jeans felt intentional, a subtle nudge to stop hiding in the background.

Riley looked over from a nearby rack, her eyes landing on the jeans with a spark of approval. "Now *those* are a move," she said, grinning. "Didn't know you had good taste hiding in there."

He glanced down at the jeans. "I wouldn't have picked these a week ago."

"Growth looks good on you," she said, then nodded toward the back. "C'mon. Every good outfit needs a finishing touch."

They made their way into the accessories section. Tables cluttered with rings, stacks of bracelets, and rows of scarves surrounded a central display of sunglasses perched on tiered stands. Noah's eyes immediately landed on one pair—round frames with mirrored lenses that seemed alive with shifting colors. Blues melted into purples, purples into golds, the shades dancing under the store's soft lighting. They were completely absurd, a touch over the top, and undeniably perfect.

"You *have* to try them," Riley urged with a mischievous grin. She crossed her arms, clearly waiting for the show.

Noah hesitated for only a moment before picking them up. He slid them on and turned toward the mirror.

The world transformed in an instant—brighter and

sharper with colors blooming in vivid intensity. The edges of the room softened, but his own reflection seemed to come into sharper focus. The sunglasses didn't just frame his face; they seemed to frame an idea of who he could be. Cool. Confident. A little unpredictable.

Riley stifled a laugh, her hand covering her mouth as she watched him. "Oh, yeah," she said, her voice warm with approval. "That's *it.*"

Noah studied his reflection again. The lenses reflected just enough of the light to give him an edge, a hint of mystery. He tilted his head slightly, catching another angle, and the confidence that flickered in him earlier now burned brighter.

"It suits you," Riley said. "You, but, like, turned up a notch."

Noah nodded, a smile lingering as he took one last look at himself in the mirror. Every piece of the outfit felt like a puzzle piece clicking into place. But these sunglasses weren't just the finishing touch; they were a kind of exclamation point. Bold. Unapologetic. Complete.

With everything in hand, Noah headed toward the fitting rooms. A sales associate materialized, her short purple hair and easy smile confirmed she belonged here more than anyone else.

"Need a room?" she asked.

"Yeah," Noah replied with a faint edge of excitement.

"Right this way." She pointed and led him towards a fitting room near the back. With a quick turn of a key she opened the door and stepped aside. "Let me know if you need anything."

"Thanks," Noah said, stepping inside and shutting the door behind him.

The fitting room was cozy, lit with warm lighting that gave everything a softer edge. The neutral walls and wooden bench provided a simple backdrop, making the colors of his selections pop. Noah carefully hung each item on the hooks, stepping back to take them in.

He started with the graphic tee, slipping it over his head. The fabric was snug but comfortable, the electric streaks of color standing out vividly against his skin. It was different from anything he'd worn before, but instead of feeling strange, it felt *right*. Next, he slid into the jeans. They fit perfectly, hugging his frame just enough, but not restrictive.

Finally, Noah shrugged into the letterman jacket, the silky lining cool against his arms. As he adjusted the shoulders, he felt it settle into place like it had been made just for him. He reached for the sunglasses last, pushing them up onto his head to hold his hair back. He took a step back and faced the mirror fully.

The person staring back was familiar but different. Confident. Almost daring. The outfit didn't feel like a costume—it felt like an extension of himself, a version of Noah he'd always carried but never let out. It wasn't about hiding anymore. It was about showing up.

Noah stepped out of the fitting room. His heart raced slightly from the strange, exhilarating energy that had been building.

"There he is," she said. "The Noah I always knew was in there."

He felt a strange mix of emotions—gratitude, relief,

and a tentative kind of pride that stirred deep inside him. He'd expected to feel different in these clothes, but he hadn't realized how much it would matter to see someone else notice it too.

"How does it feel?" Riley asked as she looked him over.

Noah glanced down at himself, smoothing a hand over the jacket. "Feels... good," he said. "Like, really good."

She grinned, a spark of triumph in her eyes. "I told you," she said, nudging him lightly. "It suits you."

"Yeah, yeah," Noah said, rolling his eyes but unable to hide the growing smile on his face. "You were right."

"Always am," Riley teased.

After another glance in the mirror, Noah ducked back into the fitting room and carefully changed into his old clothes. As he folded the new outfit, a quiet sense of excitement lingered. It wasn't just fabric—this was a step forward, a way to hold onto the confidence he'd felt the moment he saw himself in the mirror.

They headed toward the counter, where the sales associate was arranging a display.

"Ready to check out?" she asked, stepping behind the register.

"Yeah," Noah said, setting the clothes down carefully on the counter. He hesitated for a moment. "I think I found exactly what I needed."

Her smile widened as she began scanning the tags. "That jacket," she said, glancing at the letterman with an approving nod. "Solid pick."

"I wasn't sure at first," he admitted, "but... it

feels right."

The sales associate paused for a moment and glanced at him. "That's kind of the point, isn't it? Clothes don't make you someone else—they just help you show what's already there."

Noah nodded, the words settling in his chest. "Yeah," he said after a beat. "I guess you're right."

"That'll be sixty-three dollars and fifty-seven cents," she said, giving him a quick smile.

Noah handed over the cash, grateful that this kind of reinvention came with a thrift-store price tag. It wasn't about the money—it was about what it represented. He'd taken a leap today, and this was the moment it became real.

The associate handed him the bag. "Enjoy your evening," she said. "And for what it's worth? You're going to turn some heads in that jacket."

"Thanks," Noah said shyly, glancing at Riley. She rewarded him with a smile.

Stepping back outside, Noah was greeted by the crisp early evening air. The sun had begun its slow descent, casting a warm, golden hue over the city streets. Shadows stretched longer, and the air took on that unmistakable mix of cooling pavement and distant barbecues.

Riley glanced at him with a mischievous grin. "Alright, Harper, let's see it," she said, nodding at the bag in his hand.

Laughing, Noah pulled the sunglasses out and slid them onto his face. He struck a playful pose, tilting his head slightly to one side. "What do you think?"

Riley clapped her hands. "Oh, absolutely. You're

ready to steal the show. Tonight's going to be something to remember."

He met her gaze, his heart pounding with a mix of excitement and nervous anticipation. There was a truth in her words. Like tonight was a marker, a line he was crossing without realizing it.

"But we're not done yet," Riley continued. "Come on—there's still more to explore."

They strolled through the winding streets, venturing into corners Noah would usually avoid—places where energy and life spilled out onto the pavement. Snippets of conversation blended with bursts of laughter from open café doors, and street musicians filled the air with music that seemed to dance between the notes of the city itself.

They wandered into a farmer's market that stretched along a closed-off avenue. Vibrant tents lined both sides, vendors displaying a variety of fresh produce, handmade jewelry, eclectic artwork, and trinkets that seemed plucked from a storybook. The air was thick with the mingling aromas of funnel cakes, roasting chestnuts, and spiced cider.

Noah paused at a stall showcasing a series of bold, swirling paintings. Each piece seemed to reach out with its own story, the colors spilling across the canvas.

"Look at that," Riley remarked, standing beside him. "It's impressive how much someone can say without a single word."

"Yeah," Noah said, his gaze lingering on a piece that depicted a swirling galaxy against abstract shapes. "Feels like they're putting a part of themselves out there."

She turned toward him, her expression softening into something more thoughtful. "Kind of like you're doing tonight."

He looked back at the painting, then at Riley, offering a faint smile. "Maybe," he said. "But it's different. This is art. I'm just…" He trailed off, unsure of how to finish the thought.

"You're still figuring it out," she said simply, giving him a nudge. "And that's okay."

The artist stood nearby, arranging prints on a collapsible table. Noah pointed to the swirling galaxy piece.

"Did you paint this one?"

The artist nodded. "Yeah. That one's called *Resonance.*"

Noah hesitated, then said, "It's... really something. Feels like it's breathing."

The artist smiled. "That's the goal."

As they moved on, Riley leaned in. "You know that was kind of poetic, right?"

He rolled his eyes. "Accident."

They passed a booth where a vendor had set out an array of beaded necklaces, handwoven scarves, and a collection of eccentric hats. Riley beelined toward a floppy sunhat stitched with stars and crescent moons, the brim wide and dramatic.

She plucked it off the hook and placed it on her head with exaggerated grace. "What do you think?" she asked, striking a pose. "Too much?"

Noah tilted his head. The hat was absolutely ridiculous. And yet, somehow, she made it look effortless.

"You could pull it off," he said.

She grinned and gave a theatrical bow. "Maybe some other time." She placed the hat back on the rack and gave him a wink.

At a small table cluttered with enamel pins and iron-on patches, Noah picked up a tiny pin shaped like a cassette tape—pink with black spools and the words *good noise* etched along the top.

Without thinking too hard, he handed the vendor a few bills and clipped the pin to the strap of his bag.

Riley arched an eyebrow. "Impulse buy?"

He shrugged. "I like it."

She smiled. "That's allowed."

He looked down at the pin again. It was small, maybe insignificant. But it felt like a choice. A moment. Something to keep.

"Yeah," he said quietly. "I think I'm starting to understand that."

As they weaved in-between small shopfronts and glowing tents, the soft strumming of a guitar caught Noah's attention, drawing his gaze to a musician seated on a worn stool. The man's fingers moved over the strings, playing a slow version of "Every Breath You Take" by The Police. The song floated through the air.

"Wow, he's good," Riley said. She nodded toward the open guitar case at his feet. "You should toss him a dollar."

Noah pulled a loose bill from his pocket. He stepped forward and dropped it into the case. The musician looked up, nodding in thanks with a warm smile.

As Noah stepped back, Riley gave him a small, approving nod. "Nicely done," she said.

He laughed softly. "What? Being decent?"

"No," she said. "Appreciating the little things. Letting yourself stop and take it all in."

She was right—he hadn't just noticed the music. He'd felt it, like a thread tying him to the world around him in a way he hadn't before.

They kept walking, the night air cool against their skin. Riley looked up at the night sky, her breath visible in the chill. "Think we've done it all?" she asked.

"Almost," Noah replied. "But I think this was enough for one night."

"Enough for tonight," she echoed. "But not forever."

He nodded, slipping the sunglasses back onto his face, their mirrored lenses catching the faint glow of the streetlights. Riley turned to look at him, her grin widening as she took him in.

"Alright," she said, nudging his arm lightly. "You're officially pulling it off."

"Think so?" he asked, tilting his head just slightly for effect.

She laughed. "Oh, I know so. This is your look."

They walked on, the farmer's market fading behind them as twilight painted the sky in shades of pink and orange. Street lamps flickered to life, casting pools of light onto the sidewalk.

Eventually, they arrived at a small park nestled between rows of brownstone buildings. It was the kind of place that seemed almost hidden—a quiet oasis amid the urban sprawl. Benches lined a cobblestone path, and old-fashioned lampposts stood sentry, their wrought-iron designs intricate against the dusky sky.

Noah found an empty bench beneath a large willow tree, its cascading branches swaying gently in the evening breeze. He sat down with a sigh, setting his bags beside him.

"So, how are you feeling?" Riley asked, her voice soft and attentive.

He took a moment before responding.

"I don't know," he said finally. "Today has been… different. Good different, I think. But there's still this part of me that wonders if it's real. If I'm really capable of this."

"What do you mean?" Riley prompted gently.

He sighed, searching for the right words. "I guess it's just easier to blend in. Standing out—it's not something I'm used to. And today… it feels like I'm stepping into shoes that don't quite fit."

"Noah," she began, her voice full of warmth. "I think you've got it all wrong. This isn't about being someone else. It's about letting out the part of you that you've kept hidden. The part that's always been there, waiting for a chance."

He swallowed, his throat tightening. "What if I can't do it?" he asked, his voice barely above a whisper. "What if I mess it all up?"

"You won't," Riley assured him. "And even if you do, so what? That's part of living. It's okay to be scared. It's okay to mess up. But what's important is that you're trying. You're taking that first step. That's what really counts."

He closed his eyes, letting her words wash over him. It was hard to shake the doubts, but there was something comforting in her unwavering belief. "It's just... I've always been afraid of being seen. Like, really seen. I'm scared that if people notice me, they'll realize I'm not worth it."

Riley's voice softened. "You are worth it, Noah. You've always been worth it. You just haven't given yourself the chance to see that yet. But I do. I see you. And I promise, there's so much more to you than you think."

A gentle breeze rustled the leaves above, and he felt a sense of calm settling over him.

"Maybe you're right," he conceded quietly. "Maybe I need to give myself a chance."

"That's all I ask," she replied warmly. "One step at a time."

They sat in comfortable silence for a while, the sounds of the city distant and muted. The park seemed like a world unto itself.

After a few minutes of silence, Riley took a deep breath and spoke. "You know... there's something I haven't told you."

Noah glanced at her, his curiosity piqued, but he stayed silent, giving her the space to continue.

She bit her lip, hesitating for a moment, as if weighing her words. "People... people always think I have it all together, you know? Like I'm this confident, happy person who's always in control." She laughed, but it was a hollow sound, lacking her usual spark. "My parents definitely think so."

Riley, the girl who radiated confidence, who seemed fearless and untouchable, was suddenly peeling back a layer to him.

"They think I'm fine," she continued. "Every morning, I get up, go to school, smile, joke around, get good grades... They think that's proof that everything's perfect. But it's like they don't even see me, you know? They just see what I want them to see."

Noah's heart tightened. He knew that feeling all too well—the pressure to be what others expected, to blend in or stand out depending on what the world demanded.

"Have you ever... I don't know... tried telling them how you feel?" he asked gently.

She shook her head. "I wouldn't even know where to start. They're always so proud, you know? Proud of my grades, proud of the fact that I never get into trouble, that I'm responsible. And I know it sounds silly, but... I don't want to disappoint them. It's easier to just keep going, keep pretending everything's okay."

Noah nodded. He realized that Riley's confidence, her boldness, was just as much a mask as his loneliness had been. It was a shield, a way to keep the world at a distance so she didn't have to let anyone see the cracks beneath the surface.

"Sometimes I feel like I'm just going through the motions, you know? Like, if I don't keep moving, if I don't keep smiling and being this 'perfect' version of myself, everything will fall apart."

He reached over, his hand resting gently on hers. "I get it. I really do," he said. "It's hard to let people see what's underneath. Especially when they already have this idea of who you're supposed to be."

Riley looked down at their hands, her fingers curling around his. "You don't have to pretend around me, Noah. You don't have to hide anything."

He felt a rush of warmth, her words sinking deep, touching something he hadn't realized was so raw. "And you don't have to pretend around me, either," he replied, his voice barely more than a whisper.

She gave him a shaky smile, her eyes glistening with unshed tears. "Thanks, Noah. It's just... nice to feel like someone gets it, you know?" Riley let out a long sigh, her shoulders relaxing. "Sometimes, I wish I could just be honest with them. But I don't know... I'm scared they won't understand. Or worse, that they'll just brush it off."

Noah squeezed her hand gently. "You don't have to do it alone, Riley. And if you ever decide to talk to them... I'm here. I'll listen, and I'll help however I can."

A small, genuine smile broke through her sadness, lighting up her face in a way that made his heart ache. "Thank you, Noah. Really. It means a lot."

After a few moments, Riley's voice broke the quiet, tinged with playful curiosity. "So, are you excited about the party tonight?"

He laughed. "Excited and terrified."

"That's normal," she said reassuringly. "First big party?"

"First any party," he admitted.

"Well, then it's going to be extra special," she declared. "Do you have everything you need?"

He glanced at the bags beside him. "I think so. Got the clothes, thanks to you."

"Hair? Shoes? Accessories?" she listed.

He smiled. "I didn't realize there was so much involved."

"Fashion is an art," she quipped. "But seriously, you'll look great."

"Thanks," he said.

A thought crossed his mind, bringing a new wave of anxiety. "There's just one problem."

"What's that?" she asked.

"I don't know how to dance," he confessed, his cheeks warming with embarrassment.

"Ah," she responded thoughtfully. "Well, that's easily fixed."

He raised an eyebrow. "I don't think so. I'm hopeless."

"Nonsense," she countered. "Everyone can dance. It's just about feeling the music and letting go."

"Easier said than done," he muttered.

"Stand up," Riley instructed gently.

Noah furrowed his brow. "What?"

"Come on, stand up," she urged, offering her hand. "Trust me."

He hesitated, glancing around the quiet park. Even with no one else around, the request felt slightly ridiculous. But Riley's outstretched hand, patient and unyielding, finally convinced him. He took her hand and rose to his feet.

"Now, close your eyes," she instructed softly.

Noah gave a quick, skeptical look around, checking once more that they were alone. Then, with a sigh, he shut his eyes.

"Picture a favorite song," she continued. "Imagine it filling the air, surrounding you."

He inhaled, allowing the familiar strains of "Time After Time" by Cyndi Lauper to drift through his mind, filling in the silence. It was a song he'd never shared with anyone, something he reserved for private moments when he needed reassurance. The soft melody crept into his thoughts, the music warm and comforting.

"Now, let that rhythm fill you. Feel it move through you," Riley coaxed.

The opening chords of the song played vividly in his head now. The lyrics wove themselves into the moment, tender and evocative: *Caught up in circles... confusion is nothing new.* His body wanted to respond, but the stiffness of his own insecurities held him back.

"Good," Riley encouraged, her voice a steady presence. "Don't think about how you look. Just feel it, and move."

He let the lyrics guide him, the soft refrain circling in his mind: *If you're lost, you can look, and you will find me... time after time.* He shifted his weight slightly, hesitant, the imagined rhythm tugging at him. He could sense his body wanting to respond to the beat, but the stiffness of his own insecurities held him back. It was one thing to hear the music in his mind; it was another to let it guide him openly, especially in front of someone else.

"Yes," she said, with genuine approval.

He let himself sway, his shoulders loosening slightly as he began to step in time with the song. The tension gradually ebbed as he lost himself in the imagined music, the faint sound of crickets around them fading, leaving only the melody and Riley's quiet presence: *If you fall, I will catch you... I'll be waiting... time after time.* With each sway, he felt his body moving with a naturalness he hadn't expected.

"You're doing it," Riley praised.

Her words sparked a smile, unguarded and real, on his face. "This is... actually kind of fun," he admitted.

"Exactly," she said. "Dancing isn't about doing it perfectly."

He opened his eyes, still gently swaying. The park stretched out around them in the deepening twilight, trees silhouetted against the sky. Everything felt... different, as though some invisible weight had lifted.

"Now, let's try a simple step," she suggested, stepping forward to demonstrate. "To the right, then to the left. See? Just like that."

He watched her intently, the casual grace of her movements serving as both instruction and invitation. He mirrored her steps, letting her rhythm guide him, and felt his own confidence grow. The steps were simple, just shifting his weight from side to side, but as he focused on the beat in his mind, it started to feel natural, like he was part of the music.

"Add a little spin," she added playfully.

Noah attempted the spin, feeling a rush of confidence, but he stumbled, catching himself just in time. He let out a surprised cry.

"Maybe I'm not ready for that," he chuckled, shaking his head.

"Practice makes perfect," she teased back, grinning. "But it's not about perfection, remember?"

They continued for a while longer, her gentle instructions guiding him, encouraging him to experiment with his movements. His awkwardness softened, his inhibitions easing with each step. Soon, he began to exaggerate his moves—stepping with purpose, spinning in mock-dramatic fashion. Riley laughed, clapping her hands as he leaned into the silliness, each step and turn loosening him even more, his laughter bubbling up as he embraced the freedom of the moment, feeling a kind of lightness he had never felt before.

Then, as he spun back to face her, Riley stepped closer. "How about we try something together?" she suggested, extending her hand.

He blinked, and placed his hand in hers. Her touch was warm, grounding him as they stood face to face. She gave a gentle tug, leading him into a simple sway, and they moved together, shifting side to side in a slow, easy rhythm. With her hand guiding him, his nerves settled, and he found himself mirroring her steps, matching her gentle movements with ease.

"You've got it," she said, smiling up at him.

They began to add small steps, moving in sync as if they'd been doing this for ages. With each step, Riley added little spins and turns, playfully twirling under his arm, then laughing as she stepped back to face him again. He couldn't help but laugh too, surprised by how effortless it felt. The world around them faded into the background, leaving just the two of them swaying under the park's soft lights.

At one point, Riley slipped her arm around his shoulders, and he instinctively placed his hand at her waist, pulling her closer. They swayed together, barely moving now, just letting the quiet rhythm of their own laughter and breath guide them. It felt intimate yet easy, as if this dance was less about steps and more about simply being present together.

After a while, she leaned back, her eyes bright with laughter. "See? Dancing isn't so hard."

He chuckled, feeling a warmth in his chest. "Maybe not. With the right partner, anyway."

"You're a natural," Riley declared, watching him with admiration.

He let out a laugh, still breathless. "Hardly," he said, his grin widening. "But thanks."

"Anytime," she replied, her gaze warm. "Just remember, when we're at the party, don't overthink it. Feel the music and have fun."

He nodded. "I'll try," he promised.

They both sat back down, the evening quiet settling around them again. But this time, he felt a new energy, a spark that hadn't been there before.

"Do you think people will notice if I'm terrible?" he asked after a moment.

"Honestly?" she said. "Most people are too wrapped up in their own worlds to worry about others."

"I guess that's true."

"Plus," she added, a hint of mischief in her tone, "if anyone gives you trouble, just bust out those killer moves we just practiced."

He laughed. "Yeah, that'll show them."

Daylight had faded, the sky deepening to a rich indigo, stars shimmering like scattered diamonds. The lampposts cast a soft glow, illuminating the path ahead.

"We should probably head back," Riley said. "I need to get ready."

Noah nodded. "Yeah, same here. Big night ahead."

They walked together toward the edge of the park, the night air cool against their skin. The impromptu dance lingered in Noah's mind, the melody of "Time After Time" still playing faintly in the back of his head. Sharing his fears, even briefly, had lifted some of the weight he hadn't realized he'd been carrying, and the simple act of moving to music—letting himself trust the rhythm—had left him with a quiet confidence.

CHAPTER EIGHT

After parting ways with Riley, Noah made his way back to where he'd left his bike. He unlocked it, giving the handlebars a quick shake to make sure everything was in place, and swung his leg over. He pedaled onto the street, the distant hum of the farmer's market fading behind him replaced by the rhythmic sound of his tires on the pavement.

Reaching his house, he dismounted and walked his bike up the driveway. The windows glowed softly, indicating his mom was home.

He smiled to himself as he entered the house. The familiar scent of home greeted him—a blend of his mom's lavender candles and something savory cooking in the kitchen.

"Hey, Noah!" his mom's voice carried warmly from the kitchen. "How was your day?"

"Good," he called back, slipping off his shoes near the door and setting them neatly against the wall. He leaned down to grab the bags he'd tucked under his arm, careful not to bend the record or wrinkle any fabrics inside. "Really good," he added, almost to himself.

She appeared in the hallway, wiping her hands on a dish towel. Her eyes dropped to the bag he was holding, and her smile widened. "Did you get some new clothes?"

she asked, nodding toward the thrift bag.

"Yeah," Noah said, trying to sound casual. He shifted the bag to his other hand, suddenly feeling self-conscious. "Picked up a few things."

"That's great! Dinner will be ready in about thirty minutes—meatloaf, if you're hungry. Your dad's working late again."

Noah nodded, a flicker of guilt tugging at him. "Thanks, but I might eat later," he said. "I've got plans tonight."

Her eyebrows lifted, and her smile turned curious. "Oh?"

He hesitated, adjusting his grip on the bag. "A friend invited me to a party," he said.

Her expression brightened. "That sounds fun," she said warmly. "Do you need a ride?"

"No, I'm good," he said quickly. "Thanks, though."

She studied him for a moment, her smile softening. "Alright. Just be safe, okay?"

"I will." Noah turned toward the stairs, hesitating briefly. "Thanks, Mom."

He headed upstairs to his room, closing the door behind him. He leaned against it for a moment, letting out a slow breath. His gaze fell to the bag in his hand.

"Time to get ready," he thought, feeling a mix of excitement and nerves fluttering in his stomach. The thought of the party ahead—of stepping into a room full of people, of being seen—both thrilled and unsettled him. He took another steadying breath, hoping to transform the nervous energy into something closer to confidence.

He headed to shower off the day's adventure. The hot

water was a welcome comfort, steaming up the bathroom as it poured over him. As he stood under the spray, he found himself thinking about the night ahead—about Riley's confidence in him, about dancing in the park. His nerves began to untangle slightly, replaced by a cautious optimism. By the time he turned off the water and wrapped himself in a towel, the warmth had settled into him, steadying his thoughts.

Back in his room, he grabbed the TV remote from his desk and flopped onto his bed, scrolling through his streaming apps until he found the movie he'd been searching for: *Back to the Future*. He skipped ahead to one of his favorite scenes—Marty McFly shredding "Johnny B. Goode" onstage at the Enchantment Under the Sea dance.

The energy of the music and the crowd in the scene filled his small room, drawing him in. As Marty tore into the guitar solo, Noah smiled to himself, imagining what it would be like to take the stage like that—bold, unafraid, letting the music take over. He turned off the TV and set the remote back on his nightstand.

He placed the thrift store bag on his bed and opened it, pulling out the pieces of the new outfit he'd chosen so carefully. For a moment, he hesitated, his fingers brushing lightly over the fabrics. A small part of him wondered if he was trying too hard, but another part—the louder part—urged him forward.

Noah took his time dressing, his thoughts drifting back to the park. He remembered the way Riley's voice had gently guided him to let go. He smiled faintly remembering her easy laughter, the light in her eyes as she twirled under his arm, and the warmth of her encouragement when he stumbled but kept moving.

Finally, he reached for the letterman jacket, the vibrant blue catching the light as he picked it up. He held it for a moment, running his fingers over the patches sewn into the sleeves and chest. Each one felt like a small badge of rebellion, of individuality, daring anyone who saw them to notice. With a deep breath, he slipped the jacket over his shoulders. The weight of it was immediate, like armor he'd chosen for himself.

He adjusted the collar, brushing an invisible speck off the lapel as he turned to the mirror. He straightened his posture, letting his shoulders fall back slightly, and stared at his reflection.

He glanced toward his desk where a small bottle of cologne sat, half-forgotten from Christmas. He rolled it between his fingers, then spritzed a crisp mist onto his neck. He breathed it in, the faint aroma blending into the energy already building inside him.

Turning back to the mirror, he paused, taking in his reflection. His hair was still slightly tousled, loose strands falling in uneven directions. He ran a hand through it, adjusting a few pieces until they framed his face just right. His eyes moved downward, taking in the outfit as a whole. It wasn't just the clothes—it was the way they made him feel, like he was stepping into a version of himself he'd always hoped to be. He looked... different. Confident. Capable.

For a moment, he stepped back, his hands falling to his sides. The reflection staring back wasn't entirely familiar, but it felt like someone he could grow into, someone he wanted to be. A slow smile spread across his face, and with it, a quiet determination. Tonight wasn't about blending in—it was about stepping forward.

The soft buzz of his phone on the desk broke through his thoughts. He reached for it, the screen lighting up with a message from Riley: *"Ready? I'm waiting outside."*

Noah's heart skipped a beat. "It's time," he told himself. He caught his reflection one more time. "You've got this," he said aloud, nodding at himself.

Downstairs, the faint sound of the television drifted from the living room. Noah moved quickly but paused in the doorway when he spotted his mom curled up on the couch, a throw blanket draped over her lap. A cup of tea rested on the coffee table, steam curling gently upward.

She looked up when she saw him, her eyes widening slightly. "Well, don't you look sharp!" she exclaimed, a genuine smile spreading across her face. "That jacket is something else."

Noah flushed slightly. "Thanks, Mom," he said, trying to sound casual.

She stood up, walking over to him. "You look really good," she said, reaching out to straighten his jacket. "Very stylish."

"Figured I'd try something new," he said lightly. Her approval warmed him more than he wanted to admit.

"Alright then," she said, stepping back with a smile. "Don't stay out too late."

"I won't," he promised.

As he opened the front door, the cool evening air greeting him. He paused on the porch, taking in the scene before him. The neighborhood was quiet, the distant hum of traffic the only sound breaking the silence. He spotted Riley waiting by the curb, her silhouette framed by the glow of the streetlamp. She wore bright jacket to match his—a mix of blue and red, bold even in the dim light. Her hair fell loosely around her shoulders, with a single strand tucked behind her ear, catching the glint of a small star-shaped earring. She wore scuffed high-tops and a casual tee beneath her jacket, her look was effortlessly cool and a little rebellious. When she noticed him, she flashed a grin.

"There you are!" she called out. "I was starting to think you were going to chicken out."

He rolled his eyes but couldn't suppress the smile that tugged at his lips. "Not a chance," he said.

Her eyes sparkled with excitement, reflecting the light like twin stars. "That's what I like to hear," she said, giving him an approving nod. "You look fantastic, by the way."

"Thanks," he said, feeling a surge of pride. "You weren't kidding about the jacket."

"Told you it would suit you," she teased. "Now, come on. We've got places to be."

She grabbed his hand and led him down the sidewalk. The quiet anticipation of the night surrounded them, and Riley's steady presence beside him helped calm his nerves.

As they walked, Riley cast a glance at him. "So, on a scale of one to freaking out, how nervous are you?"

He gave her a sideways look. "Do I have to answer that?"

She laughed, bumping her shoulder against his.

"Relax, Harper. It's just a party. People are going to love you."

He hesitated, the confidence he'd been building starting to falter. "What if I don't know anyone there? Besides you, I mean."

Riley waved a dismissive hand. "You'll see people that know you. You're not as invisible as you think, you know."

"That's... debatable," he muttered, shoving his hands into his jacket pockets.

She sighed dramatically. "Okay, first rule of tonight: no self-deprecating Harper nonsense. Second rule: don't overthink. Just be your awkwardly charming self, and you'll be fine."

"Amazing pep talk," he said dryly.

"Hey, my pep talks are gold. You're lucky to have me," she shot back, grinning.

They approached the bus stop just as the bus's headlights appeared down the street, casting a warm glow as it approached.

The doors opened with a soft hiss, and they boarded, finding seats near the back. Noah settled into his seat, feeling the hum of the bus underfoot as it pulled away from the curb. Around them, a few passengers sat absorbed in their own worlds—a couple quietly talking, a teenager scrolling through her phone, an older man dozing with his hat pulled low. The lights inside the bus flickered slightly, casting everyone in a muted glow.

"Okay, let's talk strategy," Riley said, leaning toward him.

"Strategy?" he asked, raising an eyebrow.

"For surviving this party," she said. "I know you're a little freaked, so let's make a plan. First, we'll hit the kitchen. Grab a drink—it's an easy way to blend in. Then we'll scope out the scene and figure out who's worth talking to."

"And by 'worth talking to,' you mean people you already know," he guessed.

"Obviously," she said, laughing. "Don't worry, I'll introduce you. You'll be everyone's new favorite Harper by the end of the night."

He chuckled softly, some of the tension easing from his chest. Her confidence was infectious, as always. "Is there a third step to this plan, or do we just wing it after that?"

"Step three is the most important," she said, tapping her temple like she was revealing some great secret. "We dance."

Noah groaned. "Of course we do."

"Don't even start," she said, pointing a finger at him. "You're not allowed to bail on me when the music gets good."

He held up his hands in mock surrender. "Fine, fine. I'll try not to embarrass you."

"Impossible," she shot back, smirking. "But I'll take what I can get."

The bus continued on, winding through dimly lit streets lined with quiet houses. The soft, golden glow of porch lights spilled onto empty sidewalks, and windows flickered faintly with the blue hue of televisions inside. Noah leaned his head against the cool glass of the window, watching as the familiar landscape blurred into streaks of light and shadow. Each passing street felt like a small step farther from the comfort of routine and closer to something unknown.

Noah's thoughts wandered. His nerves began to ease, lulled by the bus's gentle rocking. He took a slow, steadying breath, letting the tension in his chest soften.

The bus slowed as it approached a stop, the brakes hissing softly, and Riley turned to him, her gaze catching his. "Almost there," she said.

Noah nodded, pulling himself upright as the bus gently jerked to a halt. The doors hissed open, letting in a burst of cool night air that carried the faint sound of laughter and distant music. Together, they stepped off the bus, the cold biting against his skin and making the collar of his jacket feel more snug, more protective.

Noah looked down the block, his gaze settling on the house just a few doors away, where strings of lights crisscrossed the front porch and spilled warm light across the yard. The thumping bass of the music vibrated in the air, a steady beat that pulsed with the thrill of the night. A few people lingered outside, talking in small groups, their voices and laughter adding to the energy building around them.

"Alright, Harper," she said, turning to face him fully. "This is it. You ready?"

He took a deep breath, letting the weight of the moment sink in. Meeting her gaze, he nodded, feeling a surge of confidence. "I'm ready."

Her grin widened. "Good. Let's make tonight unforgettable."

As they crossed the yard, Noah's stomach twisted. He

wasn't sure if it was nerves or excitement—or maybe some messy combination of the two. The music grew louder with every step, the steady pulse of the bass vibrating faintly underfoot.

They made their way up the driveway. Lanterns on the porch cast a welcoming light, and the open door invited them in, the sounds of laughter and lively conversation drifting out to greet them.

Riley walked beside him, her presence reassuring. "Remember," she said softly. "Just be yourself. That's more than enough."

He smiled appreciatively. "Got it."

Inside, the atmosphere was electric. The living room had been transformed into a makeshift dance floor, with furniture pushed against the walls to make space for the crowd. A DJ was set up in one corner, nodding his head to the beat as he mixed tracks. Colored lights swirled overhead, casting shifting patterns across the walls and floor.

Noah blinked, taking it all in. The music thrummed in his chest and the mix of voices creating a chaotic but oddly energizing hum. Riley, as usual, navigated the space like she owned it, weaving through the crowd.

"This is... a lot," he admitted, leaning closer to her so she could hear him over the noise.

She laughed. "It's supposed to be! Don't worry, you'll get the hang of it." She gestured toward the hallway. "Come on, drinks are this way."

They weaved through the throng of partygoers, Riley leading the way. Noah followed closely, trying to avoid bumping into anyone.

They reached the kitchen, which was slightly less crowded but still bustling with activity. The room was spacious, with sleek countertops and stainless-steel appliances. A large island in the center held an array of drinks and snacks. Bowls of chips and platters of finger foods were interspersed with soda bottles and pitchers of various concoctions.

"Looks like they've got quite the setup," Noah remarked.

"Indeed," Riley agreed, leaning casually against the counter. "Why don't you grab us something refreshing?"

He offered a small smile. "Any preferences?"

"Surprise me," she said with a wink.

Noah stepped up to the island, navigating around a couple who were deep in conversation. He picked up two cups and surveyed the options. Opting for something simple, he poured a citrus punch from one of the pitchers. The scent was tangy and sweet.

As he placed the lid back on the pitcher, he felt a light tap on his shoulder. Turning, he found himself face-to-face with a tall guy wearing a backward baseball cap and a friendly grin.

"Hey, man," the guy said, his tone friendly and upbeat. "That jacket? Absolute classic. Like something straight out of an 80's movie."

Noah felt a flush of both surprise and pleasure. "Oh, thanks," he replied, glancing down at his jacket. "I guess that's kind of what I was going for."

"Well, you nailed it," the guy laughed, raising his plastic cup in a mock toast. "I'm Trevor, by the way."

"Noah," he introduced himself, lifting his own

cup slightly.

"First time at Jake's?" Trevor asked, leaning against the counter.

"Yeah, actually," Noah admitted. "Figured I'd check it out."

"Good call," Trevor said, nodding appreciatively. "He throws the best parties. Always a good time."

Noah took a sip of his drink. "So, you know Jake well?"

"Yeah, we're on the soccer team together," Trevor explained. "He's a cool guy. Hey, if you want, we're starting a game of pool in the den later. You're welcome to join."

"That sounds fun," Noah said, genuinely considering the offer. "Maybe I'll swing by."

"Awesome," Trevor replied. "See you around." With a friendly pat on Noah's shoulder, he melted back into the crowd.

Noah turned to find Riley watching him with a satisfied smile. "Already making friends?" she remarked, taking one of the cups from him.

He shrugged modestly, but couldn't hide the smile that tugged at his lips. "Yeah, I guess so. Trevor seems nice."

They clinked their cups together before taking a sip. The punch was crisp and invigorating.

They lingered in the kitchen for a while, leaning against the counter as they observed the ebb and flow of people. A group nearby was debating the merits of classic rock versus modern pop, while another cluster laughed over a shared joke.

Noah found himself relaxing, the initial sense of overwhelm fading as he acclimated to the atmosphere. He glanced at Riley, who was watching the scene with an amused expression.

"What?" he asked, raising an eyebrow.

She shook her head lightly. "Nothing. Just happy to see you enjoying yourself."

He smiled softly. "It's not as scary as I thought it would be."

"Told you," she teased gently.

After a few minutes, Riley nudged him. "Alright, enough standing around. Let's check out the dance floor."

He followed her gaze to the living room, where the music had shifted to an upbeat track that had people moving enthusiastically. The dance floor was alive with motion—bodies swaying, hands in the air, laughter mingling with the melody.

Noah hesitated, the old apprehension creeping back. "I don't know," he began.

She rolled her eyes playfully. "Don't think so much. Remember our dance in the daylight? Just feel the music and let go."

Before he could protest further, she grabbed his hand. "Come on," she urged, pulling him gently toward the throng.

He allowed himself to be led as Riley navigated them through the moving crowd. The pulse of the music grew louder the closer they got to the center, where the lights dimmed and vibrant beams sliced through the air, painting the room in bursts of color. The energy hit him like a wave, electric and impossible to ignore, as if the room itself was alive and breathing in time with the music.

Riley turned to face him, her body already moving in sync with the rhythm. She tilted her head toward him. "Just follow my lead."

Noah hesitated for a moment, the crush of bodies around him making him acutely aware of his own movements—or lack thereof. He nodded. The music thudded in his chest, the vibrations settling somewhere deep, urging him forward. Slowly, cautiously, he began to move, his steps small and unsure, testing the waters.

Riley spun once, her movements effortless, her laughter ringing out like a thread cutting through the noise. She wasn't just dancing—she was part of the music, her body a living instrument attuned to the beat. Noah couldn't help but admire the way she gave herself to it so completely, her confidence radiating outward. It wasn't long before the energy of the room started to chip away at his self-consciousness, pulling him in like a magnet.

He let his shoulders loosen, his arms find their place in the rhythm. The beat was insistent, urging him to move faster, bigger, freer. Riley reached out to him briefly, giving his hand a light tug before spinning away again, her laughter infectious.

As the song's tempo built, Noah began to match it, his steps growing bolder. His body moved instinctively now, the music guiding him. The lights above strobed in bursts of red, blue, and yellow, illuminating the faces around him. The room was alive, a swirling mass of sound, light, and movement, and for the first time, he felt like he belonged in the center of it.

Riley looped back toward him, her arms raised as she swayed to the beat. "Not bad!" she shouted over the music, her eyes sparkling.

Emboldened, he tried a more exaggerated move—a playful spin that nearly sent him into someone's shoulder. He caught himself just in time, apologizing with a shy smile. Riley grinned, stepping closer to steady him, her laughter making the whole thing feel less embarrassing and more... fun.

The song shifted gears, sliding into a slower groove. The tempo eased, but the rhythm remained steady, drawing out smoother movements from the crowd. Noah felt his breathing slow as the energy shifted, the flashing lights softening to a more ambient glow. Around them, couples began to pair off, their movements fluid and close.

Riley leaned toward him, brushing a stray strand of hair from her face, her breathing slightly heavy from the dancing. "How you holding up?" she asked.

He nodded, a grin still tugging at his lips. "Surprisingly good."

She laughed softly. "Told you dancing wasn't so bad."

Noah rolled his shoulders, still moving slightly to the slower beat. "It's... not what I expected," he admitted. "In a good way."

"Need a break?" Riley asked.

He nodded. "Break sounds good."

They found a quieter spot near the wall, watching as people flowed past. The music thumped on, the energy of the party showing no signs of fading.

Just then, Lily from his History class approached, a friendly smile on her face. Her auburn hair was pulled back in a loose braid, and she wore a floral dress that complemented her warm complexion.

"Hey, Noah," she greeted, her eyes bright. "I thought that was you out there."

He straightened up, a bit surprised. "Oh, hey, Lily. Yeah, that was me attempting to dance."

She laughed lightly. "Well, you looked like you were having a great time. I don't remember seeing you at these kinds of scenes."

He shrugged modestly. "Trying something new."

"That's awesome," she said genuinely. "Maybe we can dance together later?"

He glanced nervously at Riley before replying, "Sure, I'd like that," feeling a flutter of excitement.

"Great! I'll see you around," she said, giving a small wave before disappearing back into the crowd.

Riley raised an eyebrow, a sly smile on her face. "Look at you, Mr. Popular."

He chuckled, a bit sheepish. "Sorry, I wasn't really thinking—I didn't expect someone else would ask me to dance."

She nudged him playfully. "Don't worry, I'm not the jealous type. And give yourself some credit—you're making connections."

He considered her words. "Yeah, I guess I am."

Noah watched the lights flicker across the faces around him. And for once, he didn't feel out of place. He turned to Riley, who was still grinning, her eyes reflecting the lights above. Whatever came next, he wasn't standing on the outside anymore.

CHAPTER NINE

Noah and Riley drifted away from the dance floor, the bass-heavy music fading behind them as they moved through the house. The hallway they entered was lined with framed photos and small pieces of eclectic artwork. Noah's eyes darted to the pictures as they passed—a mix of family portraits, candid snapshots, and abstract pieces. It felt strange, walking through someone else's life displayed on the walls, but it added a human touch to the party's chaos.

They turned a corner and stepped into the den where the energy spiked again. Groups of people gathered in tight clusters, animated with laughter and conversation. The clatter of foosball handles caught Noah's attention first—a group of four was locked in a heated match, their shouts cutting through the room.

Nearby, a large flat-screen TV mounted on the wall glowed brightly, displaying the vibrant chaos of *Mario Kart*. A couple sat on the edge of a low couch, leaning forward. The screen showed the iconic Rainbow Road track, its twisting, colorful paths the race neared its final lap.

A guy in a backwards cap mashed the buttons on his controller, his kart swerving dangerously close to the edge of the track. "Come on, come on!" he muttered under his breath as Donkey Kong sped toward a row of item boxes. He snagged a red shell just as his opponent, a girl playing as Yoshi, zoomed past him with the aid of a golden mushroom.

"No way you're beating me!" she shouted, her fingers deftly flicking the joystick to dodge a stray banana peel.

As they neared the finish line, Donkey Kong fired off the red shell, sending Yoshi spinning off the track in a dramatic tumble. "Yes!" the guy yelled, jumping slightly as his kart crossed the finish line just seconds ahead of hers.

The small crowd gathered behind them erupted in cheers and groans. "Finally!" one of his friends called out, clapping him on the shoulder. The girl threw her hands up in frustration before breaking into a laugh. "Alright, alright, you got me," she said, tossing her controller onto the couch.

Noah glanced at Riley, who raised an eyebrow at him. They exchanged a quick laugh.

Then Trevor appeared through the crowd. "Noah! There you are. We're about to start that pool game if you're still interested."

Noah turned to Riley who gave him an encouraging nod. "Yeah, count me in," he replied.

"Awesome. Come on," Trevor said, motioning for him to follow.

They wove their way to the far end of the den, where a sleek pool table stood under a low-hanging lamp with a green shade. The warm light cast a soft glow over the polished felt surface, and a small group of people had gathered, dividing into pairs and grabbing cues from a nearby rack.

Noah found himself paired with Lily, who gave him a cheerful smile. "Looks like we're partners," she said.

"Guess so," he replied, feeling a pleasant mix of nerves and excitement.

Riley lingered nearby, leaning casually against the wall. "I'll be cheering you on," she said.

Trevor grabbed the chalk, spun it on the tip of a cue, and handed it to Noah. "Break us off, man," he said, stepping back with a grin.

Noah steadied himself. He lined up his shot, positioning his hand on the table and drawing the cue back slowly. With a focused nudge, he sent the cue ball speeding forward. It struck the triangle of balls with a sharp *crack*, sending them scattering. One of the solid balls rolled into a pocket with a satisfying thunk.

A small cheer rose from the group. "Nice shot!" Lily said, giving him an approving nod.

"Beginner's luck," Noah replied, grinning despite himself.

Mike, a tall guy with a mischievous grin and a knack for commentary, leaned on his cue like a sportscaster. "Alright, Noah, let's see what you've got," he teased, gesturing dramatically toward the table. "The future of this match hangs in the balance!"

Noah leaned over the table for his next shot, aiming carefully. The cue ball tapped a ball, sending it rolling just shy of the pocket. A mix of groans and laughter rippled through the group.

"Almost had it!" Lily said, laughing.

"Just warming up," Noah shot back, chuckling as he moved aside to let the next player take their turn.

As the game unfolded, the atmosphere lightened. Each round seemed to dissolve more of his initial hesitation. When someone else narrowly missed a shot, Noah joined in the good-natured teasing, feeling a genuine connection to the group's easygoing energy. Riley caught his eye from across the room and gave him a thumbs-up, her grin saying it all. The longer the game went on, the more he felt himself leaning into the moment, letting go of the shyness that so often kept him on the sidelines.

When his turn came again, Noah focused on a bank shot. He lined it up carefully, angling the cue ball toward the rail. The ball ricocheted perfectly, striking a solid and sending it into the side pocket. The group erupted into cheers, and Mike threw a hand in the air. "Now *that's* how it's done!" he declared, clapping Noah on the back.

Noah grinned, his confidence buoyed by the energy of the room. It felt good—better than he'd expected.

As the game neared its end, it came down to the eight-ball. Noah crouched low over the table, gripping the cue tightly as everyone around him fell silent in suspense. He aimed carefully. With a steady strike, the cue ball sailed across the table, tapping the eight-ball and sending it straight into the corner pocket. The thunk of the ball dropping was followed by a burst of cheers and groans from the group.

"Victory!" Lily declared, throwing her arms up dramatically and ruffling Noah's hair with a laugh.

Noah laughed, his face warm with pride. He couldn't

help but feel a surge of accomplishment.

Trevor clapped him on the shoulder. "Great game, man. Glad you joined in."

Lily shot him a playful look as she leaned her cue against the rack. "You sure you're not hustling us? Beginner's luck doesn't usually last that long."

Noah chuckled, shaking his head. "I promise, this is as good as it gets."

"Modest too," Mike added with a wink.

As the group began to disperse, Riley crossed the room to him, tucking her arm lightly around his. "Look at you, Mr. Pool Shark," she teased. "I'm almost impressed."

"Almost?" he said, raising an eyebrow.

"Let's not get carried away," she replied with a laugh, nudging him toward the doorway.

Together, they slipped back into the flow of the party, the music and chatter growing louder as they moved through the lively rooms. Conversations overlapped and bursts of laughter echoed off the walls. Noah felt the energy of the night wrapping around him like a current.

As they reached the kitchen, Riley peeled away, heading toward the counter to refill her drink. The kitchen buzzed with chatter and the low thrum of music seeping in from the next room. Noah leaned against the counter, the weight of the night settling comfortably on his shoulders.

"Look who's making friends," a voice broke in, sharp and unmistakable.

Noah looked up to see Todd in the doorway, arms crossed, his smirk curling with disdain. His voice carried easily over the buzz of the room, and a few heads turned in quiet curiosity.

"Didn't expect to see you here, Harper," Todd continued, loud enough for everyone nearby to hear. "Looking for some attention?" Todd's eyes flicked to the others in the room, as if inviting them to laugh along.

Noah felt his face heat, his earlier confidence dissolving under Todd's stare. He forced himself to stand his ground, keeping his voice steady. "I'm just here to enjoy myself, like everyone else."

Todd laughed, a hollow, mocking sound. "Sure, right. Acting like you're somebody now, huh?" He stepped closer, his voice dropping just enough for only Noah to hear. "We both know you don't belong here."

Noah clenched his jaw, unwilling to back down, and met Todd's stare. "I don't need your permission, Todd."

Todd's smirk lingered, his eyes narrowing as he took another slow step forward. "Is that right?" he said, his tone low, almost casual.

Noah didn't move, his pulse quickening as Todd leaned in slightly. Without warning, Todd gave him a shove. Noah stumbled back a step, his sneakers squeaking faintly on the tiled floor. The kitchen buzz fell silent as people turned to watch. The tension in the air thickened.

For a heartbeat, all Noah could hear was the blood pounding in his ears. He steadied himself, the adrenaline hitting hard as his hands curled into fists. But he didn't raise them. Instead, he straightened, glaring at Todd with a calm that surprised even himself. "You done?" Noah asked, his voice low but firm.

Todd's smirk didn't falter, but his eyes flashed menacingly. "Not even close," he said, stepping closer again. "What? You think you're tough now? Gonna do something about it?"

Noah wanted to shove Todd back, to knock that smirk clean off his face. "I don't need to prove anything to you."

Todd's smirk faltered slightly, his bravado cracking under the weight of Noah's reply. "Yeah, that's what I thought," he said. He glanced around the room, realizing the crowd wasn't as entertained as he'd hoped.

Someone in the back muttered, "What's his problem?"

Todd's shoulders stiffened, his expression twisting into frustration. "You think you're better than me?" he snapped suddenly at Noah, his voice louder. "You're not. You're nothing."

Noah exhaled slowly, steadying himself. He felt the heat of everyone's eyes on him. "I don't think I'm better than anyone," he said evenly. "But I know I'm not nothing."

Todd took a menacing step towards Noah. Suddenly Trevor stepped in between them, pulling him back. "Alright, cool it, man," he said. "Take it somewhere else. No one's here for this."

Todd glared at Trevor, yanking his arm away with a frustrated growl. His face twisted with anger as he threw one last glare at Noah. "This isn't over," he muttered before turning sharply and shoving through the crowd, disappearing into the noise of the next room.

Breathing heavily, Noah looked over at Riley, her

eyes wide with concern. He could feel people's eyes on him, some whispering, others just watching. His pulse slowly settled, replaced by a strange mix of embarrassment and a simmering anger.

Trevor glanced around the room, then back at Noah. "You good?" he asked.

Noah nodded, his breathing steadier but his fists still flexing at his sides. "Yeah. I just didn't expect it to... go there," he admitted.

Trevor leaned slightly against the counter. "Todd's got a habit of picking fights, man. He's all bark most of the time, but I'll admit, he looked like he was pushing it tonight." He paused, then added, "You kept it together, though. A lot of people would've swung on him, and that would've just made it worse."

Noah hesitated, the simmering anger still stirring somewhere beneath the surface. "I don't know," he said, his voice low. "Feels like I just stood there and let him take his shots."

Trevor shook his head, giving a small chuckle. "Trust me, you didn't. You standing there and not letting him rattle you? That's a win, dude. The second you start throwing punches, that's when he wins. That's what he wants."

Noah managed a small nod. "Thanks," he said quietly.

Trevor clapped him lightly on the shoulder. "No problem. Just don't let it mess with your night. Todd's not worth it." He gestured toward the rest of the room, where the buzz of conversation and laughter was steadily returning. "There's still plenty of party left. Go enjoy it."

With that, Trevor gave him a quick nod and moved off toward a group by the drinks. Noah exhaled, feeling the tension finally beginning to ease, though a dull ache lingered in his chest.

"Hey." Riley's voice broke through his thoughts as she stepped up beside him. Her expression was cautious, but her eyes carried the warmth he'd come to rely on. "You okay?"

Noah gave her a faint smile, nodding. "Yeah. Just needed a second."

Riley tilted her head slightly, studying him. "You sure? Because I saw the way Todd got in your face, and I know that's not easy to just brush off."

Noah leaned back against the wall, letting out a shaky breath. "It wasn't easy," he admitted. "I wanted to hit him. But I didn't."

"And that's the difference," she said simply. "You didn't."

He let that sit for a moment, then glanced at her. "Still doesn't feel great," he admitted. "It's like no matter what I do, he's always there to remind me I don't fit here."

Riley frowned, leaning against the wall beside him. "You really think that?"

"Yeah," he said, shrugging. "I mean, Todd's not subtle. And half the time, I feel like everyone else is thinking it, even if they're not saying it."

Riley's brow furrowed. "Noah, no one's thinking that. Most people didn't even notice until Todd started yelling. And the ones who did? They saw you stand your ground. That's what they'll remember."

Noah glanced around, catching a few glances from

people nearby. But the moment had already passed, fading into the background noise of the party.

Riley nudged his arm lightly. "Look, Todd's Todd. He's always going to try to make someone else feel small because that's how he makes himself feel big. But the fact that you're here? You're already ahead of him."

A small smile tugged at the corner of Noah's lips. "You think so?"

"I know so," Riley said. "And you handled him better than most people would. You stood up for yourself without stooping to his level. That's not easy to do."

Noah exhaled, feeling the knot in his chest ease just a little more. "Thanks, Riley. I needed to hear that."

She gave him a grin. "What are friends for?"

He straightened, rolling his shoulders back as the weight of the confrontation faded. "Alright," he said, his voice a little stronger now. "Let's make tonight count."

Riley's grin widened. "That's more like it." She gestured toward the patio doors. "Come on. Let's get some fresh air."

With one last glance around the kitchen, Noah followed her. They stepped out into the cool embrace of the backyard. Strings of paper lanterns hung overhead, strung between tree branches, their soft golden light spilling over the patio and yard. The warmth of the lanterns contrasted with the crisp night air, creating a cozy, almost magical atmosphere. The sound of laughter mingled with the occasional chirp of crickets, and the low hum of conversation seemed to fill every corner.

In the middle of the yard, a fire pit blazed, its flames crackling and licking the air, sending faint sparks skyward like tiny fireflies. A small crowd gathered around, the warm glow drawing them in like moths. Some perched on low stools, others leaned casually against the backs of chairs, their laughter mingling with the gentle hum of the night. The firelight danced across their faces, painting them in warm hues of gold and orange, shadows flickering and shifting with the movement of the flames.

The sweet, smoky aroma of toasted marshmallows wafted through the air, mixing with the earthy scent of pine trees. Someone held a stick carefully over the fire, the marshmallow at its tip puffing up and browning. A sudden yelp broke through as another stick's marshmallow caught fire, the owner waving it frantically before blowing it out to the sound of lighthearted jeers and laughter from the group.

Someone began strumming a guitar. The murmurs quieted slightly, and a few people turned to listen. The fire pit seemed to draw everyone closer together, the shared warmth and light creating a sense of intimacy.

Riley nudged Noah gently with her elbow. "Want a marshmallow?" she asked.

Noah grinned faintly. "I think I'll pass," he said. "Let's find someplace quiet."

They wandered farther into the yard. The lantern's glow dimmed slightly as they moved toward the edges where the light filtered softly through the trees. At the far end, tucked into a corner, they found a small stone fountain. The water trickled quietly over smooth rocks, its sound soothing against the backdrop of laughter and crackling fire. Flowering shrubs surrounded the fountain, their blossoms gently swaying in the night breeze.

Noah and Riley exchanged a glance, their silent agreement leading them to a wooden bench near the fountain. They sank into it, the bench creaking faintly beneath their weight. For a moment, they sat quietly, the energy of the party giving way to the tranquil rhythm of the fountain.

Riley leaned forward, dipping her fingers into the cool water of the fountain. She traced small, lazy circles on the surface, her gaze thoughtful as she looked around. "This is nice," she murmured, her voice soft, as though speaking any louder might shatter the peace of the moment.

"This place is incredible," Noah remarked, gazing around.

"It really is," Riley agreed. "And you're fitting right in."

He smiled thoughtfully. "You know, I always thought scenes like this weren't for me. That I'd feel out of place."

"And now?" she prompted.

"Now, I feel like I belong," he admitted. "It's a good feeling."

"What's been your favorite part so far?" Riley asked, turning toward him with an easy smile.

Noah paused, thinking it over. "You mean besides running into Todd?" he replied dryly.

"Ha, ha," she said, rolling her eyes but grinning.

"Honestly? Just… being here. Experiencing it all. Dancing, meeting new people, stepping out of my comfort zone."

She nodded approvingly. "That's what life's about—

collecting moments like these."

Noah was about to respond when a voice called out from behind him. "Noah, right?" He turned to see Jake, the host of the party, walking up to them with an easy grin. "Having a good time?" Jake asked.

"Yeah, it's been great," Noah replied, surprised by how naturally the words came out. He extended his hand, and Jake clasped it in a solid handshake.

"Awesome, man", Jake said with a smile. "I just wanted to let you to know I heard about Todd. That guy's out of here—I told him to take a hike. Hope he didn't ruin your night."

Noah blinked and managed a small smile. "Thanks, Jake. I appreciate it."

"No problem. Make yourself at home," he said before moving on to greet another group.

As Jake drifted away, Riley nudged him with an amused smile. "See? Even Jake knows who you are."

Noah shook his head as he looked around, taking in the faces and the energy around him. "Guess I'm not as invisible as I thought," he said.

Riley laughed, her eyes scanning the room. "Invisible? Hardly. I've been telling you, Noah—you're way more interesting than you give yourself credit for."

He hesitated, rubbing the back of his neck, before his gaze shifted. "Honestly? I think it's because of Todd."

Riley's smile faded slightly, replaced by a thoughtful look. "What do you mean?"

"Think about it," he said with a short laugh. "If Todd hadn't caused a scene, no one would've noticed me tonight."

Riley shook her head firmly. "No, that's not true. You were already making an impression before Todd decided to show up with his ego. People are noticing you, Noah, because you're actually letting them see you. That's all you."

He nodded. "Maybe," he said.

Riley smiled, nudging him gently. "Not maybe. Definitely. You're here. You're part of this. And from the looks of it, you're doing pretty great."

Riley's eyes scanned the yard with a mischievous glint. "You know what we have to do next?" she asked, her voice carrying just enough intrigue to pique his curiosity.

Noah raised an eyebrow, "What's that?"

"You'll see," she replied, grabbing his hand and pulling him toward the house with an eager laugh.

CHAPTER TEN

As they stepped back inside, the sound of the party hit them like a wave. Riley's eyes lit up as she spotted the source of the commotion— a small platform in the next room, complete with a microphone and a karaoke machine. A crowd had gathered, cheering and laughing as someone enthusiastically belted out a pop song, slightly off-key.

"Karaoke," said Riley, a mischievous look on her face.

Noah let out a nervous laugh, looking at the crowd by the mic. "You really think that's a good idea?"

She shrugged, leaning in with a grin. "I think it's a great idea. You've come this far, haven't you?"

He looked back at her, half-amused, half-terrified. "I'm not exactly known for my, uh… vocal talents."

"Even better," she said, nudging him. "No one's expecting you to be the next rockstar. Just go up there, have a blast. Trust me, they'll love it."

He shook his head, still uncertain but warming to the idea. "And if I completely mess it up?"

Riley laughed. "Even better."

He took a breath, the hint of a smile creeping in. "Alright. But if I bomb, you owe me a drink."

"Okay, but seriously, what's your go-to song? Everyone has one," Riley asked, her eyes glinting.

Noah frowned, giving a small shrug. "I don't know. I usually just listen, not perform."

"Well, that's about to change." Riley stopped him just before the platform, turning to face him directly. "Close your eyes."

"What?" He raised an eyebrow, skeptical.

"Just do it," she insisted with a grin.

Noah sighed but complied, shutting his eyes.

"Now, think of a song that makes you feel something. Like... one that gets stuck in your head because it just hits right. Something you'd sing if no one else was listening."

Noah let the noise around him fade as he tried to focus. A song? One the *meant* something? Too many came to mind all at once—scattered from half-memories attached to different times. Nothing stuck. But then, almost by accident, one came through a little clearer than the rest.

He opened his eyes. "I think I've got it."

Riley clapped her hands, beaming. "Then let's do this."

They stepped together toward the song selection screen. Noah scrolled through the extensive list, his thumb hovering until it landed on the one. A smile tugged at the corner of his mouth as he selected "Don't You Forget About Me" by Simple Minds. It was a song he'd always connected with—a timeless anthem that felt fitting for the moment.

The current performer finished their song to a smattering of applause, bowing slightly before stepping down and offered microphone to Noah.

Stepping onto the small platform, Noah's palms felt damp against the mic. He swallowed hard, his heart pounding in his chest as the opening chords began to play. The familiar melody filled the room, and a hush fell over the crowd. All eyes turned toward him.

For a moment, Noah's nerves threatened to overwhelm him, but as his gaze swept across the room, he spotted familiar faces. Lily leaned against the back of a chair, her hands clasped in anticipation. Trevor and Mike stood off to the side, nodding to the beat, their smiles genuine. And then there was Riley. She gave him a small nod, her eyes shining with encouragement.

The first notes of the lyrics tumbled from his lips, shaky and barely above a whisper: *"Hey, hey, hey, hey... Ooh, woah..."* The sound felt foreign, tentative, and a couple of murmurs rippled through the back of the room. His grip on the mic tightened, his throat constricting as the nerves fought to take hold.

Then someone clapped—one person, clear and deliberate. Maybe Riley. It broke through the tension like a crack of lightning. A breath he didn't realize he was holding escaped, and he pushed forward. By the next line, his voice steadied: *"Won't you come see about me? I'll be alone, dancing, you know it, baby..."* The familiar words settling into him.

As the first verse gave way to the chorus, something inside him shifted. He caught Riley's eye again, grounding him. He let go of the tightness in his shoulders, the words coming smoother now, stronger: *"Don't you... Forget about me... Don't, don't, don't, don't..."* The music swelled, and so did his confidence.

By the second verse, Noah felt something he hadn't expected: freedom. *"Will you stand above me? Look my way, never love me..."* The crowd swayed gently. He moved a little with the rhythm, letting the beat guide him.

When he reached the second chorus, something incredible happened. A few people in the back started clapping along to the beat. Then grew, spreading through the crowd like wildfire. By the time he hit the next line, *"Don't, don't, don't, don't... Don't you, forget about me,"* someone else joined in, their voice weaving into the melody, and then another, until a small unplanned chorus filled the room.

Noah felt a wave of energy rush over him as the crowd's momentum picked up. Friends threw their arms around each other, swaying to the beat, their voices blending with his in a harmony that was messy but beautiful.

"Will you walk on by? Will you call my name?" His voice rang out clear, steady, the nerves replaced with a sense of exhilaration. He swayed with the rhythm, his confidence growing with every note. He didn't care how he looked, didn't care about whispers or laughter.

By the final chorus, the energy in the room was electric. *"I sing, La, la-la-la-la, la-la-la-la, La-la-la-la-la-la-la-la-la-la..."* The voices around him grew louder, rising with his. The crowd wasn't just watching anymore; they were part of it. Noah leaned into the mic, his voice breaking slightly but full of emotion: *"When you walk on by... And you call my name!"*

As the final note rang out, Noah's chest heaved with the effort, his pulse racing like he'd run a marathon. He lowered the mic, the weight of the moment catching up to him all at once. A beat of silence followed, a collective inhale from the crowd.

And then the applause erupted, a tidal wave of cheers and whistles that filled the room, crashing over him in a way that made his chest swell with something he could only describe as pure joy. He laughed, the sound unrestrained and unguarded, as if the sheer exhilaration of the moment had nowhere else to go.

As Noah stepped off the platform, the party seemed louder now, the adrenaline in his chest making everything feel sharp and alive. Before he could take a breath, Lily appeared.

"That was insane!" she said, grinning. "How are you just casually good at that?"

Noah gave a sheepish laugh, rubbing the back of his neck. "I don't know. I wasn't even sure I could do it."

Trevor joined them, a wide grin on his face. "Man, I thought you were gonna blow it, but you were solid. Full rockstar mode."

Noah shook his head, but he couldn't help the smile forming. "It was just one song. Let's not get carried away."

"So, are you up for a dance?" asked Lily.

Noah glanced over to Riley, who smiled, giving him a nod.

He turned back to Lily. "Count me in," he said.

They made their way to the living room, where the music pulsed and colored lights flickered against the walls. People laughed and moved to the beat, the floor alive with motion.

Moving to the rhythm as they settled into the throng, Noah felt more at ease than he had all night. The nerves, the doubts—everything were melting away, leaving just the music, the lights, and the thrill of the moment.

"You know," Lily said, leaning in slightly as they danced, "you've surprised a lot of people tonight."

Noah glanced at her. "How so?"

She tilted her head, smiling. "I think most people didn't really notice you before."

He let out a quiet laugh, shaking his head. "That's not surprising. I've spent a lot of time trying *not* to be noticed."

Lily raised an eyebrow. "Why's that?"

He hesitated. "I don't know. It just feels... safer. When no one sees you, they can't judge you."

Her brow furrowed slightly. "I get that, but... isn't it kind of lonely too?"

He looked back at her, something in her voice making him pause. "Yeah," he admitted after a beat. "It is."

She smiled, a little brighter this time. "Well, tonight, I noticed. And I like what I see."

Noah laughed softly, her words catching him off guard. "Thanks," he said. "I'm happy you asked me to dance."

They kept dancing, the space between them narrowing. Lily moved with an easy confidence, unfussy and relaxed. Noah followed her lead, surprised by how quickly he found the rhythm—and how good it felt not to overthink it.

"You're pretty good at this," Lily said.

Noah chuckled. "Don't jinx it. I'm one wrong step

away from disaster."

"Oh, please. You've got moves," she countered, spinning once before meeting his gaze again. "You sure you haven't been hiding out at dance studios after school?"

"Busted," he joked, raising his hands in mock surrender. "You caught me. I'm secretly a professional."

She grinned. "That would explain a lot. What other talents are you hiding?"

Noah shrugged, a playful glint in his eyes. "Wouldn't you like to know?"

"Hmm," she said, tilting her head as if sizing him up. "I'll figure it out eventually. I have to say, tonight's been full of surprises."

The low hum of the music wrapped around them, creating a bubble where time seemed to slow. The sway of their movements felt natural, effortless, as though they'd been doing this for years instead of minutes. Noah found himself relaxing, letting the moment sink in.

As the song came to an end, Lily tilted her head toward him. "Mind if we step outside for some air?"

"Not at all," Noah replied. He followed her through the crowd, weaving past small groups and toward the back deck.

It was quieter outside, the faint murmur of the party fading into the background. Overhead, the stars sparkled against a wide, dark sky.

Lily leaned against the wooden railing, her arms crossed loosely in front of her. "This has been one of the best nights I've had in a long time," she confessed.

"Same," Noah admitted, moving to stand beside her.

He rested his hands on the railing, the worn wood smooth beneath his fingers. "I wasn't sure what to expect when I decided to come tonight."

"What made you change your mind?" she asked, glancing at him.

He hesitated. "Honestly? I almost didn't. I'm not really the party type."

"Could've fooled me," she said with a teasing smile.

He smiled back. "I guess I just… felt like it was time to try something different."

Her smile softened. "Well, I'm glad you did. This night wouldn't have been the same without you."

Noah looked down, his fingers brushing over the edge of the railing. "I'm glad I did too," he said.

For a moment, they simply stood there, the stillness of the night settling around them. The faint rustling of leaves in the breeze mingled with the distant sounds of the party, but out here, it felt like they were in their own little corner of the world.

"Would you maybe want to hang out sometime? Just us?" she asked.

Noah blinked, surprised by the question. He smiled, the answer coming without hesitation. "I'd like that."

"Great," Lily said, her smile widening to match his. She shifted slightly, pulling her phone from the pocket of her jacket. "Here, let me give you my number."

Returning inside, the atmosphere was as lively as ever. Trevor caught sight of them near the doorway and waved them over to a group gathered.

"Hey, we're starting a game of charades. You guys

in?" he asked, raising his voice slightly to be heard over the noise.

"Absolutely," Noah replied, glancing at Lily, who nodded enthusiastically.

They joined the circle, and Trevor handed out small slips of paper with phrases written on them. A bowl sat in the middle of the table filled with crumpled suggestions.

"Alright," Trevor announced, clapping his hands together. "Two teams. Winners get bragging rights, losers... well, losers are just losers."

The group quickly divided, and Noah found himself on a team with Lily, a girl named Maya, and two others he recognized from school. As the game kicked off, the room buzzed with laughter, cheers, and the occasional groan as each player took their turn.

When it was Noah's chance, he stepped into the center of the circle. His slip read "Indiana Jones," and after a brief pause, he launched into his attempt. He mimed cracking a whip, ducking, and swatting at imaginary obstacles, his exaggerated gestures drawing laughter.

"Indiana Jones!" Maya called out, clapping her hands as the team erupted into cheers.

As the game continued, the competition grew more intense but remained lighthearted. Noah found himself fully immersed, caught up in the infectious energy of the group. The shared laughter, playful ribbing, and the little victories of each correct guess creating a sense of connection. Each round seemed to bring him closer to the group.

At one point, Lily took her turn, acting out *Jaws* by

pretending to swim in panic before miming a shark attack. Noah and the rest of the team shouted guesses, their voices overlapping, until he finally yelled, "Jaws!" just as the timer buzzed.

Trevor declared a break, and the group began to scatter. Noah wandered toward the kitchen and grabbed a plate, savoring the moment of quiet amidst the lingering buzz of the party.

As he munched on some chips, Riley appeared beside him.

"Having fun?" she asked, smiling.

He nodded, smiling back. "More than I expected."

She glanced around, then back at him. "Quite the change from the guy who almost didn't walk in the door, huh?"

He chuckled. "Yeah, feels like a different night entirely."

"And it's only been a few hours," she added with a wink.

Noah hesitated for a moment, then looked at her. "Hey…is it cool that I'm, you know, hanging out with other people?"

She raised an eyebrow, clearly amused. "Are you serious? Noah, this is your night as much as mine. You don't need my permission."

He gave a small, relieved laugh. "I guess I just didn't want to, I don't know, abandon you or something."

She shook her head. "Please. Have fun. I'll be around."

He nodded, feeling reassured. "Thanks, Riley."

Then, without warning, the music cut off, the sudden

silence sweeping over the crowd. A few confused murmurs rippled through the room, but they quickly gave way to cheers and laughter when Jake jumped onto the karaoke platform, a red solo cup in one hand and the microphone in the other.

"Alright, everyone, listen up!" he announced as he raised his arms to quiet the crowd. "We're about to kick this up a notch."

The room quieted.

"Time for the freestyle contest! That's right—jokes, raps, poems, whatever you want. Improv only, and the crowd decides who wins!"

A ripple of excitement passed through the crowd. A few people groaned in protest, while others cheered, already volunteering their friends.

Jake grinned, pointing toward a group near the front. "Who's got the guts to go first?"

A girl with bright pink hair stood near the edge of the room, her lips curling into a mischievous grin. "Logan!" she shouted, pointing at the guy beside her. He froze, mid-sip of his drink, his wide eyes darting around as though searching for an escape route.

"Wait, what? No!" Logan protested, shaking his head. The crowd, sensing his discomfort, began to cheer and chant his name. "Lo-gan! Lo-gan! Lo-gan!"

Pink Hair nudged him forward, practically shoving him into the center of the room.

"Fine, fine!" Logan groaned, holding up his hands in mock surrender. The crowd whooped as Logan grabbed the mic from Jake, who was already laughing. He cleared his throat. "Alright, alright," he said, holding up a hand for silence, his tone dripping with mock seriousness. He gazed dramatically into the crowd. "This one's from the heart."

Without warning, he flung his arm out theatrically and bellowed, "BA-BA-BA-BABY!" His voice cracked on the first syllable, sending ripples of laughter through the crowd. "You're my SUNSHINE on a cloudy TUESDAY! My spaghetti in a world of FROSTED FLAKES!"

Laughter erupted, but Logan pressed on, undeterred. He strutted across the room, one hand clutching the mic, the other clutching his heart. "Your LOOOOOVE is a LASERBEAM, and I'M THE TARGETTT!"

As the lyrics poured out, Logan's movements became increasingly over-the-top. He whipped his imaginary hair, dropped to his knees, and reached toward the ceiling as if calling out to an unseen deity. "YOUR TOUCH IS A TORNADOOOOO, and I'M THE MOBILE HOME!"

The crowd was losing it now, cheering and howling with laughter. Logan paused for dramatic effect, wiping an imaginary tear from his. "But alsoooooo… YOU'RE THE PICKLE ON MY BURGERRRR!" His voice wavered, his knees wobbling like he might collapse under the sheer emotional weight of his words.

"And I'M THE TOASTED BRIOCHE BUNNNNNN!" he howled, ending on a dramatic falsetto that cracked spectacularly.

At this point, people were crying with laughter. As the applause thundered, Logan stood, wiping an imaginary bead of sweat from his brow and tossing his "hair" back. "Thank you, thank you," he said, bowing deeply. "I'll be signing autographs by the punch bowl."

The room was in hysterics, applause and cheers erupting from every corner. Logan stood, taking a series of exaggerated bows before handing the mic back to Jake.

"Ladies and gentlemen," Jake said, "let's hear it for Logan and… whatever *that* was."

The crowd erupted again, some doubling over with laughter.

"Alright, that's the energy we're looking for!" Jake said. "Who's next?" He scanned the crowd, his eyes landing on Noah. "Alright, Harper. Time to shine."

The crowd erupted into playful chants of "Noah! Noah!" as his face turned crimson. He shook his head, trying to deflect. "No way."

"Come on!" Riley urged, nudging him.

Jake joined in, pointing a dramatic finger at Noah. "The crowd has spoken. Harper, the stage is yours!"

Noah hesitated, his heart hammering in his chest. He glanced at Lily, who gave him an encouraging nod. Finally, he sighed, stepping forward.

"Fine," he said, his voice wry. "But don't expect too much."

The crowd whooped and clapped as Noah took the mic. Jake clapped him on the shoulder. "Give us your best shot, man."

Noah stepped onto the platform, glancing out at the sea of faces. His mind raced, scrambling for something— anything—that might work. Then, an idea struck him, ridiculous enough to make even him laugh inside.

He cleared his throat, taking a moment to think, and stood up straighter. "Ladies and gentlemen," he began.

"Tonight, I present to you a tragic tale—a tale of heartbreak, betrayal, and loss. I call it... 'The Spill.'"

The room erupted in laughter and applause, and Noah raised a hand, silencing the crowd. "Thank you, thank you. But please... this is serious."

As the laughter subsided, he launched into the piece, his voice low and dramatic:

"Our tragedy began like any other day—
Sunlight through my blinds, chasing dreams away.
I shuffled to the kitchen, half-asleep,
Dreaming of the coffee, rich and deep.
Oh, the coffee, my salvation, my muse!
I thought nothing that day I could lose.
But fate... oh, fate... had other plans,
For tragedy struck by my own hands."

He paused, letting the silence hang heavy before continuing:

"A wobble, a slip, a clatter, a crash!
The mug hit the floor with a deafening smash.
And there it was, my morning brew,
Sprawled across the tiles—a liquid tomb."

The crowd roared with laughter, someone shouting, "Nooo!"

Noah raised his hand dramatically:

"The betrayal! The anguish! The caffeine denied!
My very soul wept; oh, how I cried!
I knelt there, in the mess, despairing and mute,
As the puddle of coffee soaked into my boot.
And so I learned, my friends, a truth profound:
Life is fleeting; joy cannot always be found.
For even the sweetest cup can shatter,

Leaving us to question… what does life matter?"

He ended with a dramatic flourish, bowing low as the room erupted into cheers, whistles, and applause. Someone shouted, "Encore!"

Jake stepped forward, laughing as he took the mic. "That… was a masterpiece."

As Noah stepped down, his heart was pounding, but a grin tugged at the corners of his mouth. He made his way back to Riley, who was laughing so hard she had tears in her eyes.

"You're ridiculous," she said, placing her hand on his chest. "But that was amazing."

"Ridiculous is right," he said, though the rush of adrenaline left him feeling exhilarated.

He glanced back at the stage, still catching his breath. Part of him couldn't believe what he'd just done—and part of him couldn't wait to do it again.

CHAPTER ELEVEN

The night had hit its stride, the buzz of the party reaching a comfortable high. Noah found himself leaning against the counter in the kitchen, laughing at Trevor.

"Okay, but seriously," Trevor said, pointing a chip in Lily's direction, "the idea that *Return of the Jedi* is better than *The Empire Strikes Back* is just peak bandwagon nonsense. I mean, Ewoks, people. Ewoks."

Lily rolled her eyes, crossing her arms. "Oh, come on. Ewoks are adorable and resourceful. You're just mad they upstaged your precious lightsabers with sticks and rocks."

Trevor threw his hands up, as if the weight of the galaxy was on his shoulders. "Adorable doesn't win battles, Lily. They should've been wiped out in two seconds. And don't even get me started on the logistics of their tree village. One Stormtrooper sneeze and it all comes down."

Lily raised an eyebrow, unimpressed. "You're really going to defend a franchise that has a guy get eaten by a sandpit with teeth?"

"That sandpit is iconic," Trevor shot back. "The Sarlacc is a metaphor for—"

"It's a metaphor for bad CGI," Lily interrupted.

Noah smiled, watching the two of them go back and

forth. The debate was clearly spiraling into ridiculous territory, but neither seemed inclined to back down.

"You're both wrong," Mike chimed in as he stepped into the kitchen. "The best part of *Star Wars* is podracing in *The Phantom Menace*. No contest."

Trevor and Lily both turned to him, faces frozen in a mix of horror and disbelief.

"Take that back," Trevor said, his tone dead serious.

Mike grinned, clearly enjoying the chaos he'd unleashed. "What can I say? It's a masterpiece. A visual symphony of speed, danger, and emotion. Perfect movie building blocks."

"It's a glorified NASCAR race in space," Lily shot back, throwing her hands in the air. "No plot, no point, just a bunch of CGI noise."

"You guys have no vision," Mike said, shaking his head in mock disappointment. "Podracing is Lucas' magnum opus."

Noah laughed so hard he nearly spilled his drink.

He was about to jump into the debate when an explosive—*BANG! BANG! BANG!*—thundered against the front door, slicing through the party like a crack of thunder. The heavy pounding reverberated through the walls, silencing the room in an instant. Conversations stopped mid-sentence, and every eye turned toward the door as the echo hung in the air.

Noah felt his stomach tighten. Conversations died down almost instantly, replaced by nervous murmurs.

"Uh-oh," Jake muttered as he appeared through the kitchen door, looking visibly uncomfortable. "Cut the music."

The bass-heavy beat that had been thumping through the house moments ago faded out, leaving an eerie silence in its wake. The tension thickened as Jake made his way toward the front door.

"Who do you think it is?" Riley whispered, leaning closer to Noah.

"No idea," he whispered back, his mind already racing through worst-case scenarios.

Maya shot a glance toward them, mouthing, "Cops?"

"Crap," Lily mouthed. Her gaze returned to the door, and Noah could see her gripping her phone tightly.

The door creaked open, and a voice boomed from the porch. "Good evening, Mr. Thompson. Someone want to explain what's going on here?"

Noah froze. That voice was familiar. Too familiar. A moment later, Mr. Hargrove, their vice principal, stepped into the house. He was still wearing his ID badge, though it hung slightly askew, and his arms were crossed in a way that immediately made Noah feel like he was back in school.

"Oh no," Riley muttered under her breath. "It's *him.*"

Mr. Hargrove took a moment to survey the room, his sharp eyes moving over the crowd. The whispering had stopped entirely; now there was only the sound of people shifting uncomfortably.

"Mr. Thompson," Mr. Hargrove said finally, his tone heavy with disapproval. "Would you care to explain why your little get-together can be heard from two blocks away?"

Jake cleared his throat. "Uh… sorry about that, Mr. Hargrove. We didn't realize it was that loud."

"Didn't realize?" Mr. Hargrove repeated, his eyebrows arching. "Jake, it's midnight. If I hadn't been out walking my dog, I wouldn't have believed the racket for myself."

Noah felt the air in the room shift as a few people started inching toward the back door, clearly hoping to slip out unnoticed.

"This is bad," Riley whispered. "Someone's gotta say something."

"Jake's handling it," Noah hissed back, though Jake's awkward stammering didn't inspire much confidence.

Mr. Hargrove shook his head. "This isn't the first time I've had to deal with this, Jake. Your house parties are becoming a neighborhood tradition—and not the good kind." His eyes narrowed. "Where are your parents, by the way? Are they even home?"

Jake hesitated. "Uh, they're out of town," he admitted, rubbing the back of his neck.

Mr. Hargrove raised an eyebrow. "Out of town, huh? And they just happened to leave you in charge?"

"Yeah, but it's not like—" Jake started, but Mr. Hargrove cut him off with a raised hand.

"I see," Mr. Hargrove said, his voice heavy with disapproval. "Well, I'll make sure to have a word with them when they get back. I'm sure they'll be thrilled to hear about this." His tone carried a sharp edge of sarcasm that made Jake shrink slightly. He opened his mouth to respond, but no sound came out. He glanced around the room, clearly hoping for backup, but most people were avoiding his eyes.

That's when Riley elbowed Noah sharply in the ribs.

"Do something," she whispered.

"What?" Noah's voice cracked slightly, and he winced. "No way."

"Come on!" she urged, somewhere between a plea and a command. "You're good with words, and Jake's sinking fast."

Noah swallowed hard, his heart pounding as he realized Riley wasn't going to let this go. The room had gone quiet again, all eyes on Mr. Hargrove. Summoning every ounce of courage he could muster, Noah stepped forward.

"Uh, Mr. Hargrove," he began.

The adult turned, his stern gaze locking onto him. "And you are?"

"Noah Harper," he said quickly.

Recognition flickered across Mr. Hargrove's face, though it did nothing to soften his expression. "Ah, Harper. Quiet kid."

Noah nodded, resisting the urge to shrink under the weight of the moment. "Uh, yeah, that's me. Listen, we're really sorry about the noise. We didn't mean to disturb anyone."

"You didn't *mean* to?" Mr. Hargrove repeated. "Because from outside, it sounded like you were hosting a rave."

Noah let out a nervous laugh, his eyes darting around. "Okay, fair point. But we'll turn everything down, promise."

Jake shot him a look, but Noah ignored it, keeping his focus on Mr. Hargrove.

"And who put you in charge?" Mr. Hargrove asked,

re-crossing his arms.

Noah shifted his stance slightly before answering. "No one, I guess," he admitted. "I just thought it might be easier to hear it from someone who gets where you're coming from. We didn't mean to cause trouble."

Mr. Hargrove raised an eyebrow, studying him for a long moment. "Here's the thing, Harper: good intentions don't excuse bad decisions."

Noah nodded, holding his gaze. "You're right. We'll keep it down. People are already starting to leave, and we'll make sure it doesn't get any more out of hand."

Mr. Hargrove sighed, rubbing his temple as though the night had been far too long already. His gaze swept over the room again, landing briefly on the empty cups scattered across the counters and a group of teens huddled awkwardly in the corner, clearly hoping to avoid notice.

"See that it doesn't," he said, his voice quieter now but no less sharp. "Because if I hear so much as a whisper, I'll be back. And next time, I won't just be talking to you. I'll be talking to all your parents as well."

He let the warning hang in the air for a moment before stepping further into the room. "And while we're on the subject, let me make one thing clear: I get it. I remember what it's like to be young, to feel like the rules don't apply to you. But this?" He gestured toward the crowd and the remnants of the chaos scattered around the house. "This isn't just about you. You've got neighbors who have kids trying to sleep, people who have to get up early in the morning—people who don't need to deal with your nonsense."

A ripple of murmured apologies spread through the room, but Mr. Hargrove wasn't finished. "You're not just a group of kids blowing off steam. You're a community. And being part of a community means thinking beyond yourselves."

Mr. Hargrove's gaze landed back on Jake. "And you, Mr. Thompson—you're the host. That makes you responsible for everything that happens under this roof. Next time you might want to think about who you're inviting. You're lucky I'm the one standing here and not the police."

Jake nodded quickly, looking chastened. "I understand. It won't happen again."

"Good," Mr. Hargrove said curtly. "Alright. I'm going to give you a chance to turn this around. Start shutting it down. Now."

With that, he straightened and moved toward the exit, pausing only to glance back one last time. "And Harper— consider using that voice of yours more often. You might be surprised what it can do."

Noah exhaled slowly as Mr. Hargrove stepped outside, the door closing behind leaving a silence so thick it felt like the air had been sucked out of the room. The tension lingered for a beat before Riley let out a low whistle.

"That was… intense," she said.

"Dude," Jake said, clapping Noah on the back. "You just saved my ass. Thanks." He clapped his hands together, breaking the momentary awkwardness. "Alright, people. You heard the man. If you don't live here, it's time to head out. I don't need my parents hearing about this from Mr. Hargrove."

Groans rippled through the crowd, but most people complied, clearly unwilling to tempt fate.

Trevor sauntered over holding a half-empty cup and looking far more relaxed than he had during Mr. Hargrove's visit. "Okay, but seriously—how did you do that without your voice cracking? I thought I was going to pass out just watching you."

"I was too scared to think about it," Noah admitted, laughing. "I just… said whatever came to mind."

"Well, it worked," Trevor said, raising his cup in a mock toast. "To Harper, the unexpected hero of the night, saving Jake's ass."

Noah chuckled. "I don't think that's how I'd describe it."

"A group of us are meeting up at the diner tomorrow for lunch," said Trevor. "You should come."

"I'd like that," Noah said.

"Awesome. See you then," Trevor said with a nod before disappearing into the thinning crowd.

For a moment, Noah stood still, absorbing the scene. It felt surreal, like he was seeing it from the outside now—a moment he wasn't sure he'd belong to again once he left. A night so far removed from the quiet, predictable rhythm of his usual life, yet somehow one he'd managed to step into, however briefly. He let that thought settle, a strange mix of pride and disbelief flickering through him.

"You coming?" Riley's voice pulling him back. She was already halfway out the door, pulling her jacket tighter against the cool night air. Her eyes caught his, a small, knowing smile lighting her face.

"Yeah," Noah replied.

Outside he hesitated once more, looking back at the glow of the party before turning to follow her. They walked down the driveway, the world outside feeling unnaturally quiet. Noah took a deep breath, letting it fill his lungs.

They walked in silence for a few moments, the moon casting a soft glow over the empty sidewalk. The quiet was peaceful, but Noah's thoughts were anything but as he replayed the night in his head.

"Penny for your thoughts?" Riley finally asked.

He smiled faintly. "Just replaying the night in my head."

"But?" she prompted, sensing the hesitation in his voice.

He sighed, searching for the right words. "I don't know. It's just… now that it's over, I feel…" He trailed off, struggling to articulate the feeling within him.

"Empty?" she offered gently.

"Yeah," he admitted. "Empty."

Noah paused, turning to face her. "Is that normal?" he asked.

"Sometimes," she said. "Sometimes after a big high, there's a low. It's like a pendulum swinging."

He considered this, nodding slowly. "Maybe that's it."

"Or maybe," she continued carefully, "you're realizing that the night was amazing, but it doesn't fix everything."

He looked at her. "What do you mean?"

She offered a small smile. "You had fun, you overcame your anxiety, and that's fantastic. But it doesn't change who you are deep down. It doesn't solve all the things you're dealing with."

He swallowed. "I guess I thought... I don't know what I thought."

She reached out, placing a hand on his arm. "It's okay, Noah. Growth takes time. Tonight was a big step, but it's just one of many."

He sighed, the tension easing slightly from his shoulders. "You're right. I just... I didn't expect to feel like this."

They resumed walking. "Feelings are complicated," Riley agreed softly.

He glanced at her, a hint of gratitude in his eyes. "Thanks for being here with me on my journey."

"Always," she replied with a gentle smile.

The houses they passed were dark, their windows like silent watchers in the shadows. Noah found himself breathing more deeply, his thoughts clearing with each step.

After a few minutes, Riley looked over at him, a playful glint returning to her eyes. "So, karaoke superstar, what's your next big move? Joining a band? Touring the country?"

He laughed softly, shaking his head. "I think one performance is enough for me."

"Oh, come on," she teased. "You can't stop now. You've got momentum."

He rolled his eyes, but his cheeks warmed at the memory. "Okay, maybe it wasn't terrible."

"It was brave," she said, her tone softening. "You were brave tonight."

The sincerity in her voice caught him off guard. He glanced at her, the glow of a nearby streetlight catching in her hair. "Thanks," he said quietly.

They kept walking, their footsteps echoing softly along the sidewalk. After a moment, Riley broke the quiet with a grin. "Okay, highlight of the night? Jake's face when Mr. Hargrove showed up. He looked like a deer in headlights. And then you stepped in, all calm and collected. It was like watching someone tame a wild animal."

"Calm and collected? Me?" Noah said, grinning. "Pretty sure I was shaking the whole time."

"Maybe, but no one else noticed," she said.

Eventually, they reached his house. The porch light glowing softly, casting a warm halo over the front steps. Noah stopped, turning to face Riley.

"Thanks for everything tonight," he said. "I don't think I could've done it without you."

Riley shrugged. "Remember, tonight was a step forward. Don't be too hard on yourself for feeling a bit down now. It's normal."

Noah nodded. "I'll try to keep that in mind."

"Good," she said. "Now go get some sleep. You've earned it."

He managed a genuine smile. "Goodnight, Riley."

"Goodbye, Noah," she replied, and turned to walk down the sidewalk. He watched her figure gradually disappear into the shadows.

He entered his home quietly, mindful of the late hour.

He paused in the entryway, slipping off his shoes and setting them neatly by the door before heading into the kitchen.

The house was still, the hum of the refrigerator the only sound. His mom had left a note on the counter: *Hope you had fun. Leftovers in the fridge. Love you.*

He opened the fridge, peering inside until he spotted the container of leftovers. He popped it into the microwave and leaned against the counter, pulling out his phone.

Notifications blinked across the screen—group photos from the party, a few new followers, even a message from Trevor: "Diner tomorrow. Don't flake."

He smiled faintly, tapping a quick reply before scrolling through the photos. There he was, mid-laugh, caught in a candid shot beside Lily. Another showed him on the karaoke platform, arms outstretched mid-song. He couldn't help but smile.

The microwave beeped. He grabbed the warm container and sat down at the kitchen table. Between bites, he scrolled through more photos from the party. Someone had posted a video—just ten seconds of him singing, but the sound was decent. The crowd's cheers came through loud and clear. He watched it twice, then locked his phone and set it aside.

The kitchen was dim except for the small light above the stove. Outside, a car passed, headlights cutting across the window and vanishing just as fast. He wiped his mouth with a napkin and brought the empty container to the sink.

He clicked off the kitchen light on his way out and

made his way upstairs, the quiet creak of each step the only sound in the house.

In his room, he shrugged off his jacket, draping it over the back of his chair. His eyes drifted to the worn posters on his walls. Tonight, they felt different—not just remnants of a world he admired, but reminders of something he could reach for. Something he could be a part of.

He thought back to the jacket as he'd tried it on at the thrift store—the way its weight had felt like more than just fabric. Wearing it wasn't just about looking different; it was a choice to step out of his comfort zone. That small decision had set the tone for everything that followed.

He remembered Riley's laughter as they danced in the park, her teasing breaking through his hesitation. Her encouragement had been a constant, gently pushing him forward when he might have stopped himself.

Sitting on the edge of his bed, he ran a hand through his hair and let out a soft sigh. Lying back, he stared at the ceiling. A subtle smile lingered as he murmured, "Things are going to be different from now on."

The words carried a quiet certainty. They weren't just a fleeting hope—they felt real, like the first steps of a shift he could feel deep inside. For a moment, he thought he heard Riley's voice. *"I think so too,"* Riley seemed to whisper in his ear. He smiled.

His thoughts turned to tomorrow, imagining himself sitting with Trevor, Lily, and the others at a table crowded with laughter and conversation. For once, he didn't feel like an outsider. The invisible wall that had kept him at a distance felt like it was finally starting to fall away.

He turned onto his side, the weight of the day settling over him. There was a quiet satisfaction in his tiredness, a sense that he had earned this moment of stillness. And beneath it all, a flicker of something else lingered: anticipation. Hope. The promise of more days like this, more moments where he could feel alive and present. And it didn't feel like an ending. It felt like the start of something new.

CHAPTER TWELVE

Noah woke up to the soft glow of morning sunlight filtering in through his bedroom curtains. He stretched, his body pleasantly aching from all the dancing and excitement.

Pushing himself out of bed, he grabbed a hoodie and slipped it on before heading downstairs, his stomach grumbling in anticipation of breakfast. He felt light, almost buoyant, as he stepped into the kitchen. It had been an incredible night. He felt different, more alive.

His mom stood by the stove, flipping pancakes, while his dad sat at the kitchen table, sipping his coffee and scanning the Sunday newspaper. Noah shuffled in and slid into a chair at the table.

"Morning," he said, and gave his parents a sleepy grin.

His dad looked up over the rim of his coffee cup. "Morning, kid. You're up early, considering the time you got home."

Noah chuckled, leaning back in his chair. "Yeah, I figured I shouldn't waste the whole day. Last night was… different."

His mom glanced over her shoulder from the stove. "Different how?"

"I don't know," Noah said, shrugging lightly. "Just… good. Better than I thought it would be."

His dad lowered the newspaper slightly, raising an eyebrow. "What, you actually had a good time?"

"Yeah, I guess," Noah replied, smiling faintly. "It was overwhelming at first. I mean, there were so many people, and I felt kind of... out of place."

His mom turned back to the stove, nodding thoughtfully. "That's how these things usually start. So, what made it better?"

"I don't know. I think I just decided to go with it," Noah said. "Riley kept nudging me to join in, and instead of overthinking it, I did. I danced. I sang karaoke—"

"Karaoke?" his dad interrupted. "You?"

Noah laughed, a little sheepishly. "Yeah. It was terrifying at first, but then people started singing along, and it felt... incredible."

His mom's smile widened. "That's amazing, sweetheart. It sounds like you really stepped out of your shell."

"I guess I did," Noah said. "It's weird—I always thought being the center of attention would feel awful, but it didn't. It felt... freeing."

His dad nodded, a thoughtful look crossing his face. "It's a good feeling, isn't it?"

"Yeah, it is," Noah said. "I spent so much time overthinking everything, worrying about how people saw me. But last night, it felt like none of that mattered."

His mom reached out, giving his hand a gentle squeeze. "I'm so glad you had that experience, Noah. And I hope you remember that feeling the next time you start doubting yourself."

"Honestly, I wouldn't have done any of it if it hadn't

been for Riley," he said.

His dad looked up from the newspaper, eyebrows raised. "Riley?" he asked. "Who's Riley?"

Noah looked up, catching his mom's eyes. He let out a small laugh, trying to brush off the sudden focus. "Seriously? I've mentioned her. She's the one who invited me to the party."

His dad set the paper down completely, leaning forward with a smirk. "Oh, sure. If you say so. But I think we'd remember."

Noah rolled his eyes, still smiling. "You guys are impossible. I know I've talked about her. You're just getting old."

His mom chuckled, crossing her arms as she leaned against the counter. "Getting old, are we? Alright, Mr. Know-It-All—why don't you tell us about her?"

Noah hesitated. "She's... she's great. Funny, really easy to talk to. She pushes me to do things I'd never think to try on my own. Last night? That was all her. And honestly... it was because of her that I had a blast."

"She sounds wonderful," his mom said warmly. "But next time, bring her by, okay? We'd love to meet her."

Noah laughed, shaking his head. "Fine, but seriously, just... try not to make it awkward."

His dad leaned back. "Awkward? Son, I've been training for this moment your whole life."

Noah groaned, dropping his head into his hands. "Why do I feel like I've just made a huge mistake?"

His dad's grin widened. "Oh, you absolutely did."

After finishing his breakfast, Noah stood up, giving his mom a quick hug. "Thanks, Mom," he said. "I think

I'm gonna go chill for a bit."

She smiled at him, patting his back. "Anytime, sweetheart. Sundays are best for lazy days."

Noah headed back upstairs to his room and closed the door behind him. He leaned back against it for a moment, letting out a long, slow breath. There was a gnawing sense of unease that had settled in his chest, and it wouldn't go away.

He pushed away from the door, crossing the room to sit on his bed. He stared at the floor, his mind replaying the conversation at breakfast. The more he tried to think about it, the more the details started to blur.

Noah closed his eyes, trying to replay the night, starting from the moment they had arrived at the party. He remembered Riley telling him to get drinks, remembered the smile on her face as she nudged him toward the kitchen. But when he tried to picture her interacting with anyone else, everything seemed vague.

His eyes flew open, his heart beginning to pound. He tried to think of specific moments where Riley had been part of the group, where someone else had talked to her, but the memories were slippery, like they were wrapped in fog. He could picture her standing beside him, smiling at him, talking to him, but no one else ever looked at her. No one else seemed to even notice she was there.

His stomach twisted, and he crossed the room to his desk. He grabbed his phone, opening the photo gallery. There had to be something—a picture, a video, some proof that she was real, that she was there with him. He scrolled through the photos from the night, his eyes scanning each one carefully. There were pictures of him, pictures of the party, of the people he had met. But Riley wasn't in any of them. Not even in the background.

Noah scrolled faster, his heart pounding in his chest, his fingers trembling. There were selfies—pictures of him smiling, his face flushed from dancing, his eyes bright with excitement. He remembered Riley standing beside him, remembered her leaning in close, her arm around his shoulder as they took the picture. But she wasn't there. Every photo was just him. Alone.

He opened his text messages, scrolling through the conversations. He remembered texting Riley. But as he scrolled, there was nothing.

Noah dropped the phone onto his desk, his hands trembling. He backed up, sinking down onto the edge of his bed, his mind spinning. He could feel his pulse in his ears, a loud, insistent thudding that seemed to drown out everything else. He closed his eyes, trying to breathe, trying to think, but all he could see was Riley's face—her smile, her eyes, the way she had always been there, pushing him, encouraging him. And now it felt like she was slipping away, like she was nothing more than a... figment of his imagination.

He opened his eyes, staring at the floor, his thoughts a tangled mess. Then it hit him—the photo booth.

The photos. The strip Riley had insisted he keep after their goofy session at the arcade. They were still in his jacket pocket. Noah shot to his feet, crossing the room again in three hurried steps. He grabbed it from the back of his chair, fumbling through the pockets until his fingers brushed against the glossy strip of photo paper.

He pulled it out, his hands trembling as he stared at

the first frame. His heart dropped.

It was just him.

Every single photo—just him. The first frame showed him staring straight ahead with an exaggeratedly serious expression. The second captured him sticking his tongue out, tilting his head dramatically. The third showed him mid-motion, his hand raised, tousling the space where Riley's hair should have been. His grin was wide and mischievous, his posture animated as if reacting to her protest. But no Riley. Not even the faintest blur or shadow. Just empty space where she should've been.

Noah blinked, his breath hitching as he turned the strip over, as if the back would hold some explanation, some proof that what he was seeing wasn't real. But the blank white paper offered no answers.

He buried his face in his hands, a sense of panic rising in his chest. He didn't understand. She had been real—so real. But if she was real, then why couldn't he find any proof that she had ever been there at all?

"Riley," he whispered, his voice barely audible in the quiet room. "Where are you?"

But there was no answer. Just silence.

Noah closed his eyes, the weight of the realization settling in his chest.

A rush of anger and confusion flooded through him. He stood and paced back and forth, his breath coming in short, shallow bursts. He clenched his fists, his whole body trembling with the intensity of it. He felt betrayed— by his own mind, by the illusion he had clung to so desperately. Riley had felt so real, so vivid. She had been everything he needed, everything he wanted to be.

Noah let out a frustrated yell. He grabbed his pillow and threw it across the room, watching as it hit the wall and fell to the floor. It did nothing to ease the pain. He wanted to hit something, break something—anything to make the ache in his chest go away.

He sank back down onto his bed, burying his face in his hands. The tears came then, hot and stinging, spilling down his cheeks. He sobbed, his shoulders shaking. He had believed in her. He had believed in every word she said, every moment they had shared. And now, it had all been a lie.

How could he have been so foolish? How could he have let himself believe in something that wasn't real? He wiped at his face and tried to steady himself.

Noah looked at the letterman jacket, lying crumpled on his bed. He had felt different wearing it—stronger, more confident. Riley had told him it would make him feel like someone new.

He clutched the jacket to his chest, his tears falling onto the worn fabric. He wanted to be angry at her. But he couldn't. Because she had been a part of him, and hating her felt like hating himself. She had been the best version of him, the version he had always wanted to be.

Noah's breath came in shaky gasps. He knew he had to accept it—had to accept that Riley had never been anything more than a reflection of his own desires, his own insecurities. But it was hard. It was hard to let go of someone who had been so real, who had meant so much to him.

He lay back on his bed, staring up at the ceiling, the jacket still held tightly in his arms. The room felt empty, too quiet, the silence pressing down on him. He tried to take a deep breath, tried to calm the storm of emotions swirling inside him, but it was like trying to hold back a flood.

Noah closed his eyes, the tears slipping down his temples, his heart aching with the loss. He didn't know how to move forward from this, didn't know how to be that confident, fearless version of himself without her. But he knew he had to try. He had to find a way to be the person Riley had made him believe he could be. Even if she wasn't real, the things she had taught him—the things she had made him feel—those were real.

Noah took a deep breath and opened his eyes, his gaze drifting toward the window. The sky was clear, the sun bright. It felt like a fresh start. He closed his eyes again, taking in a slow breath. He knew Riley wasn't coming back, not really. She had been a part of him, a part of his mind, and now that he had faced that truth, he understood that he had to move forward without her.

He opened his eyes, and she was there—Riley, leaning against the wall across the room, her arms folded, her smile soft. She looked at him, her eyes filled with that same unwavering belief she had always had in him.

"Look at you," she said, her voice gentle, almost wistful. "You're getting it now, aren't you?"

Noah smiled, his chest tightening, a mixture of emotions welling up inside him. He nodded. "Yeah," he said, his voice barely a whisper. "I think I am."

Riley pushed off the wall, stepping closer. She knelt in front of him, her smile widening. "You don't need me, Noah. You never did. Everything you did, everything you felt—it was always you."

Noah swallowed, his throat tight, his eyes stinging with tears that threatened to fall again. He reached out, his fingers brushing against hers. "I just... I wish you were real," he said, his voice breaking. "You made everything better."

Riley's smile softened, and she shook her head. "I was real in the way you needed me to be. But you don't need me anymore. You can do this on your own. You've always been able to."

Noah closed his eyes, a tear slipping down his cheek. He took a deep breath, letting her words wash over him, letting them settle into the parts of himself that still felt broken, still felt afraid.

When he opened his eyes again, Riley was gone. But the warmth of her presence lingered, a reminder of the strength she had helped him find. Noah looked down at the jacket and he nodded to himself.

He wasn't the same person he had been before. The fear, the insecurity—they were still there. But now, there was something else too. A belief in himself. Riley had helped him find it, had shown him what he was capable of. And now, it was up to him to hold onto it, to nurture it, to make it grow.

Noah stood up, slipping the letterman jacket on. He looked at himself in the mirror. He didn't look all that different, but he felt different. He felt like he was finally seeing himself for who he really was.

He took a deep breath, his heart lighter. It was time to face the world again, time to take what Riley had helped him discover and make it his own. He had found the strength within himself. And now, it was time to use it.

Noah stepped out of his front door, the sun overhead casting a warm, golden glow over the quiet suburban street. The breeze was cool against his face, prompting him to button up his jacket as he began walking down the sidewalk.

The familiar sights of his neighborhood soon gave way to the small commercial strip near the edge of town, where the diner sat nestled between a dry cleaner and a hardware store. Its wide glass windows reflected the morning light, the bold red letters of the sign above the entrance declaring "Mo's Diner" in retro font.

Even from outside, he could see them through the window—Lily talking with her hands, animated and expressive. Trevor sat beside her, leaning forward. Mike and a couple of others sat around the table, laughing at whatever story Trevor seemed to be telling.

Pushing open the glass door, the diner smelled exactly as he imagined—warm and inviting, with the comforting aromas of freshly brewed coffee, sizzling bacon, and maple syrup hanging in the air. The checkerboard tiles underfoot gleamed in the sunlight streaming through the windows, and the faint hum of a jukebox in the corner added to the retro charm.

Noah barely made it two steps inside before Lily noticed him. Her eyes lit up, and she broke into a grin, waving him over with enthusiasm.

"Noah! You made it!" she called, sliding over in the booth to make room for him.

Trevor turned as well, flashing a grin of his own. "Took you long enough."

Noah slid into the booth, offering a quick smile as he glanced around. "Hey, guys. Sorry I'm late—took me a bit to get moving today. Still shaking off last night, I guess."

Trevor laughed. "Shaking it off? Come on, man—you crushed it. That karaoke was something else."

Noah shrugged, chuckling. "Yeah, well, don't get used to it. That's not exactly my thing."

Lily smirked, leaning over. "Could've fooled me. You *actually* had the whole place singing with you."

He shook his head, smiling despite himself. "I don't know about that."

"Hey, I'm serious," Trevor said. "Getting a room full of people to join in like that? That's not easy. You've got something, man."

The waitress appeared, placing a menu in front of Noah. "Coffee?"

"Yes, please," he replied, flipping over his mug and turning to Lily. "Hey, did you happen to see me come in with someone last night? Like… at the start of the party?"

She frowned slightly, thinking. "I don't think so. Why? Were you supposed to meet someone?" Surprisingly she looked a little jealous.

Noah hesitated, running a finger around the rim of his coffee cup. "No, it's just… never mind. I thought maybe you saw me with someone when I first got there."

Lily tilted her head, watching him curiously. "Pretty sure you walked in solo. Why?"

Trevor jumped in with a grin. "Wait, Noah's keeping

secrets now? Who's this mystery person?"

"Forget it," Noah said quickly, waving them off with a small laugh. "It's nothing."

"In that case," Trevor said, leaning forward with a grin, "I think we need to address the elephant in the room. An elephant named 'The Spill.'"

Noah groaned, covering his face with one hand. "Oh, come on. Are we really bringing that up?"

"Of course I am!" Trevor said. "You get up there and pull off this perfect spoken-word thing like you're at some poetry slam."

Lily grinned, crossing her arms. "Wait, didn't you memorize that from somewhere? Because it sounded way too good to just make up on the spot."

Noah shook his head, laughing. "I swear I didn't memorize it. It just… happened."

"Just happened?" Trevor said, incredulous. "You're telling me you improv'd an entire poem about spilling coffee and somehow made it funny and deep at the same time?"

"Pretty much," Noah said with a shrug.

Trevor let out a low whistle, shaking his head in disbelief. "Okay, well now I feel an underachiever. My biggest moment of the night was my nacho tower."

Noah raised an eyebrow. "Nacho tower?"

Trevor grinned. "You should've seen it," Trevor said, holding up his hands to demonstrate the sheer height of the pile. "It was, like, an architectural marvel. Ten layers, full tilt with the works."

"Oh no," Noah said, already laughing. "Let me guess—you knocked it over?"

"Almost!" Trevor pointed dramatically at Noah. "I was doing that thing—you know when you try to grab the chip with the most toppings without disturbing the whole structure?"

"The nacho extraction technique," Mike chimed in solemnly.

"Exactly," Trevor said. "So, I go in slow, I'm committed, and then—bam! Lily bumps my elbow."

"I did not!" Lily protested.

"The top layer slid off like a landslide." Trevor continued, ignoring her. "Sour cream on the table, guac on my jeans, cheese on the floor."

Noah laughed. "Did anyone even get to eat any of it?"

"It became a tragic monument to ambition," Trevor said, placing a hand over his heart.

"Well," Lily said, flipping her hair with exaggerated pride. "Glad I could be the night's entertainment."

"Oh, you mean the photobombing?" Mike asked. "I saw at least three pictures where your head is just floating behind someone like a haunted yearbook photo."

"Four, actually," Lily said, pulling out her phone. "I've been collecting them. Behold, my greatest hits."

She swiped through a few photos—one where she was mid-blink behind Jake and Maya, another where only half her face appeared in the corner of a group shot, mouth open like she was about to yell something.

Trevor leaned over to look. "This one's incredible. You look like you're plotting to overthrow the student council."

"Unintentional mascot of the night," Lily declared

proudly. "I've accepted my role."

"I'm making you a sash," Mike said. "Like a pageant winner." That earned round of laughter.

The conversation rolled on, drifting from story to story from the night. Noah leaned back in the booth, his mug in hand, letting the voices swirl around him. He felt a sense of peace settle over him. It was the kind of afternoon that felt perfect in its simplicity, like everything had fallen into place just right.

By the time the waitress brought the check, Noah noticed something he hadn't realized before: he wasn't just enjoying himself—he felt like he belonged. He wasn't the outsider looking in anymore.

He couldn't help but smile.

CHAPTER THIRTEEN

T he school hallway bustled with activity, students rushing to their lockers, laughter and chatter echoing off the walls. Noah walked through the crowd, letting the familiar sounds wash over him. It was the same as it always had been, the same as it was every morning. But today, something felt undeniably different.

He felt different.

Noah adjusted the collar of his letterman jacket, its weight resting comfortably on his shoulders. It wasn't just a piece of clothing anymore—it was a symbol of everything he had gone through, everything he had learned about himself. Riley had told him to wear it to "look the part," but now, it wasn't about what others thought. It was a reminder that the strength he'd shown at the party—the courage to step into the spotlight and be himself—had always been inside him. The jacket wasn't magic, but it carried the memory of that night and what it had unlocked within him.

He moved through the hallway with steady, deliberate steps, his head held a little higher than usual. His eyes scanned the familiar faces of his classmates, catching a few nods and quick smiles. For once, Noah didn't look away or pretend he hadn't noticed. He nodded back with a small but confident smile. A voice called out to him as he passed a group near the lockers.

"Hey, Noah!"

He turned to see one of the guys from his English class, someone he hadn't spoken to much before. "Hey," Noah replied easily, his grin widening.

By the time he reached his locker, Noah was already riding a small wave of accomplishment. He spun the combination lock, opened the door, and began stacking his books inside when he heard someone approaching behind him.

"Yo, Noah! Cool jacket, man," a voice said, loud enough to draw the attention of a couple of nearby students.

Noah turned to see one of his classmates nodding toward him with a grin. He played it off with mock seriousness, brushing the lapel of his jacket. "Oh, this old thing? Just pulled it out of the back of the closet."

The guy laughed. "Looking sharp, Harper."

"Thanks," Noah said, the warmth in his chest growing. As his classmate walked away, Noah caught a couple of others glancing his way, their expressions friendly, curious even. He closed his locker and headed toward his first class. For the first time, the eyes on him didn't feel like judgment or scrutiny. They felt like acknowledgment.

As he walked he watched the rhythm of the hallway around him. People were moving, talking, filling the space with a buzz of energy. Usually, that energy felt like something Noah wasn't a part of, a hum that moved around him but never quite included him. Today, though, it felt different. For the first time, he felt like he was part of the current.

Just as he turned a corner, a shadow stepped into his path. Noah's heart sank as he looked up to see Todd's smirk plastered across his face.

"Well, well, if it isn't the life of the party," Todd sneered, his voice dripping with sarcasm. A couple of his friends hung back, leaning against the lockers, their smirks mirroring Todd's.

Todd gestured toward his jacket with a laugh. "What's with the new look, Harper? You trying to be somebody now?"

Noah met Todd's gaze, the heat of anger bubbling just under the surface. "I don't need to try," he said evenly, his voice steady.

Todd blinked, momentarily caught off guard by the confidence in Noah's tone. He quickly recovered, leaning in closer. "Is that right? Big shot now, huh? Think you're cool because you went to a stupid party?"

Noah felt the tension in the air thicken as a few students nearby slowed their steps, their curiosity piqued. He knew Todd was trying to provoke him, to pull him back into the timid, quiet version of himself Todd had always targeted.

But Noah wasn't that version anymore.

"I don't think I'm cool, Todd," Noah said, his voice calm but firm. "I just don't care what you think."

The words hung in the air. Todd's smirk faltered, replaced by a flicker of irritation. "Oh, really?" he said, his tone sharpening. "You've got a lot of nerve for a nobody."

Noah felt his fists clench at his sides, but he refused

to let Todd see any sign of weakness. Instead, he took a small step closer, closing the gap between them. "You're right," Noah said, his voice even and unwavering. "Maybe I am a nobody. But people can change. You should try it sometime. Then maybe you wouldn't have to act like such a jerk to feel important."

A small ripple of murmurs spread through the small crowd that had gathered. A few students exchanged glances, clearly intrigued by the confrontation. Todd's jaw tightened, his face reddening slightly as he glanced at the onlookers.

"What did you say?" Todd asked, his voice rising as he attempted to regain control of the situation.

Noah didn't flinch. He tilted his head slightly. "You heard me. Maybe if you didn't spend so much time tearing people down, you'd actually have something real to stand on."

A few scattered gasps, some students nodding in approval while others exchanged wide-eyed looks. Todd's face turned red, his jaw tightening as he looked around.

"That's funny, Harper," Todd said, his voice strained. "Real funny. You think you're some kind of big deal now?"

Noah shrugged, his hands loose at his sides. "No. I think I'm someone who doesn't have time for your crap."

Todd's eyes darted to his friends, who were noticeably quiet. The balance of power had shifted, and everyone could feel it.

"Careful," Todd warned, his voice almost a growl.

"Or what?" Noah asked. "You gonna shove me into

another locker? Steal my lunch money? Come on, Todd. Do your worst. Or better yet—don't. Just walk away. Might be the smartest move you've made all year."

Todd stared at him, his confidence clearly shaken. "You think you're better than me now?"

"No," Noah said simply, holding Todd's gaze. "I just don't think about you at all."

The crowd erupted into a mix of laughter and scattered applause. One of Todd's friends muttered, "Let's just go," but Todd didn't move.

But Todd wasn't ready to walk away. "You think you're untouchable now? A little party, and suddenly you're the king of the school?" His voice cracked slightly, the frustration seeping through.

Noah took a deep breath, feeling the weight of all the moments he'd spent shrinking under Todd's gaze, the years of letting someone else dictate how small he felt. That version of him was gone. "I'm not trying to be anything, Todd," he said. "I'm just not afraid of you anymore."

As the declaration hung in the air, Todd's face twisted in anger. He took a step forward, his hands balling into fists, one arm twitching upward as though he were on the verge of throwing a punch.

"Hey!" a voice cut in sharply. Lily stepped through the crowd, her eyes narrowing as she positioned herself beside Noah. "Back off, Todd."

Todd's bravado faltered for a split second, but he quickly masked it, turning his eyes toward her. "This doesn't involve you," he said. "Go play somewhere else, little girl."

"Oh, it does now," she shot back. "Because you're making it everyone's problem, as usual. What's the matter, Todd? Run out of jokes that don't involve making yourself look like an idiot?"

A ripple of reaction moved through the crowd—murmurs, a few muffled laughs. Todd's face flushed with irritation, and he took a step toward Lily, his posture threatening. "You think this is funny? Keep running your mouth, Lily. See where it gets you."

Now Noah stepped forward, his voice steady despite the adrenaline surging in his chest. "Leave her alone, Todd. This is between you and me."

"Oh, big words," Todd sneered, turning to face Noah. "What are you gonna do about it, Space Cadet?"

Noah didn't flinch, holding Todd's glare. "At least I know how to spell Space Cadet."

The air in the room grew heavier, the crowd quieting as Todd loomed closer. He let out a short, humorless laugh, and his hand shot out, shoving Noah square in the chest. Noah stumbled a half step back, but instead of retreating, he steadied himself and held firm, his eyes locked on Todd's.

"That's it?" Noah asked quietly, his voice calm but cutting. "That's all you've got?"

"Come on, Todd," Lily said, her voice cutting through the charged silence. "This is pathetic—even for you."

Todd turned his glare on her. "You're lucky I'm not in the mood," he spat, though his voice wavered just enough to reveal cracks in his confidence.

"Oh, I'm terrified," Lily said dryly, her arms still

crossed. "Go ahead, Todd. Show everyone how tough you really are."

Todd's gaze flicked back to Noah, then around the crowd. The weight of their stares bore down on him, and even his friends were hanging back, their expressions uncertain. Realizing he was losing the upper hand, Todd let out a bitter laugh.

"You're not worth it," he muttered, but there was no strength in his words. With one last glare, he shoved past Noah, his shoulder colliding with him hard enough to make him stumble slightly. Noah caught his balance, standing tall as Todd stormed off, his friends trailing behind.

Lily turned to Noah, her expression softening. "You okay?"

Noah exhaled slowly, the tension in his chest loosening. "Yeah," he said. "I think I am."

"Good," she said with a quick nod. "You heading to class now?"

"Yeah. You?" he asked, shifting his backpack on his shoulder.

"Same." She glanced at her phone and groaned. "Actually, I'm going to be late if I don't hustle. But hey, what are you doing for lunch?"

"Probably just eating outside like I always do," Noah replied, shrugging. "Why?"

"You should come sit with us in the cafeteria," Lily said as if it were the most obvious thing in the world. "We usually grab the table by the windows."

Noah smiled. "Alright. Lunch sounds good."

"Great," she said, already stepping away. "See you.

Don't forget!"

"I won't," he called after her, still smiling despite himself.

As he approached his classroom, Noah paused in the doorway. The noise inside spilled out into the hallway—a mix of voices, scraping chairs, and bursts of laughter. Normally, he'd slip into his usual seat without a word, keeping his head down. But today, his gaze lingered on a group of students gathered near the front of the room, their conversation animated as they joked and passed notes.

The chatter didn't pause as he entered, but he noticed a couple of glances his way. Noah's heartbeat quickened, but instead of faltering, he moved toward the group at the front and slid into an empty chair beside them.

"Hey, Noah," one of the girls said, her face lighting up with a smile. It was Jessie, someone he knew but had never really spoken to. "We were just talking about Saturday's party. You were there, right?"

"Yeah," Noah replied. "It was pretty wild."

"I thought I saw you!" she said, leaning in slightly. "You were fire on karaoke."

A faint blush crept up Noah's neck, but he let out a small laugh. "It was fun," he admitted, Riley's voice echoing in his mind.

Beside her, a boy named Matt raised an eyebrow. "Wait, you did karaoke? Noah Harper? No way."

"It's true," Jessie said, elbowing him. "And he killed it."

Matt gave Noah a nod of approval. "Alright, Harper. Didn't think you had it in you."

The bell rang, cutting off the noise as the teacher entered the room. Students settled into their seats, and Noah adjusted himself in his chair, the letterman jacket snug around his shoulders. As the lesson began, he opened his notebook and started taking notes. For once, the urge to doodle never crossed his mind.

The cafeteria was a chaotic symphony of noise—students talking, trays clattering, the hum of everyday school life. Noah stood at the edge of the room with his lunch tray, scanning the tables. Across the room, Lily caught his eye and waved him over to their group, laughter rising above the general din of the cafeteria.

He smiled and made his way to the table, sliding into an empty seat beside her. "Hey, guys," he said, his tray clattering slightly as he adjusted his seat. He felt a brief flicker of awkwardness—was he interrupting their rhythm? But the group barely paused before pulling him into the conversation.

"Alright," Lily said, pointing a fry at Maya like a sword. "You were saying?"

"I was *saying*," Maya replied dramatically, flipping her hair over her shoulder, "that there is *no way* pineapple belongs on pizza. It's like… betrayal in food form."

"It's innovation," Lily countered. "You're just too boring to appreciate it."

Noah slid his drink closer. "Pineapple on pizza? I'm for it."

Maya threw up her hands in mock outrage. "You too, Harper? Et tu, Brute? Is no one on my side anymore?"

"Connor's on your side," Lily said, gesturing to the

boy across the table, who was very pointedly eating his pizza with pepperoni and nothing else.

"Damn straight I am," Connor said, looking up with a grin. "Pineapple is an abomination. Like, just because you *can* doesn't mean you *should*."

"See?" Maya said, slapping the table triumphantly. "Thank you, Connor. At least someone understands."

"It's not about what's right or wrong," Lily argued, stealing another fry from Trevor's tray. "It's about expanding your palate. Living a little."

"You can 'live a little' without ruining pizza," Connor retorted. "What's next, frosting on a cheeseburger?"

"Actually…" Maya said, pretending to consider it. "Sweet and savory does work."

"Stop," Connor said, holding up a hand. "You're ruining lunch for me."

Noah laughed, watching the back-and-forth unfold. "Okay, but real talk," he said, leaning in. "If it's pizza and you're hungry, are you really saying no just because it has pineapple?"

Connor hesitated, narrowing his eyes. "That's a trap question."

"Exactly," Noah said, raising his drink in victory. "Food is food. Sometimes you just eat it."

"Yes," Lily said, grinning. "Noah gets it."

Maya groaned, leaning her head against her hand. "You're all monsters."

The table dissolved into laughter as Connor tried to offer Maya one of his "pure" slices as a peace offering, which she accepted, of course.

"What's everyone doing after school?" asked Trevor. "Coffee? Please tell me someone's free to save me from going home and bingeing bad TV."

"Coffee sounds good," Lily said. "Noah, you in?"

Noah paused, surprised by how naturally the invitation came. He glanced around at their expectant faces. "Yeah," he said, nodding. "I'm in."

As the group debated where to go, Noah leaned back, letting their voices wash over him. The noise of the cafeteria seemed to fade. For once the chaos felt welcoming instead of overwhelming. He wasn't skimming along the surface anymore; he was finally in the current, carried right along with the rest of them.

By the time the final bell rang, Noah was riding the momentum of the day. He walked out of the building with his hands tucked into the pockets of his letterman jacket, the sun casting a warm glow over the schoolyard. The usual crowd of students scattered across the lot, their voices blending into the hum of after-school life. Backpacks slung over shoulders, sneakers scuffing against pavement, bursts of laughter and shouts all around—it was a scene Noah had witnessed a thousand times before.

For years, he had watched it all from the sidelines, always feeling like an outsider. He would shuffle down the steps, head down, sticking to the edges of the flow, trying to get home as quickly as possible without drawing attention. But now, as he stood on the top step, he felt something entirely new—a quiet but undeniable shift deep within him. He wasn't just observing anymore. He wasn't stuck in the background, letting life move past him. He was part of the flow.

The world hadn't changed—but he had.

He lingered there, taking it all in. A group of kids were tossing a soccer ball back and forth near the bike rack, their voices raised in good-natured ribbing. A couple walked arm in arm, talking softly and smiling as if no one else existed. In the distance, someone's car alarm blared, and a burst of laughter erupted from a cluster of students sitting on a bench.

He took a deep breath and started down the steps. Making his way across the schoolyard he weaved between groups of students. A few nodded or smiled at him as he passed. He returned their smiles, a warmth spreading in his chest.

As he reached the edge of the schoolyard, Noah slowed his steps, letting the moment linger. With each step, he felt steadier, surer of the road ahead. He knew it wouldn't always be easy. There would still be days when the old doubts would creep back in, moments when fear and hesitation might feel stronger than they did now. But he also knew that he could handle them. He'd learned that strength wasn't about never feeling fear—it was about moving forward despite it.

The afternoon sun cast long shadows on the sidewalk as he made his way down the street. The coffee shop came into view, its windows fogged slightly from the warmth inside.

He reached the door and paused, his hand resting on the cool metal of the handle. The road ahead was still uncertain, filled with challenges and moments that would test him. But as Noah stood there, he felt different.

The fear hadn't disappeared entirely. It lingered, a familiar presence. But it no longer controlled him. It no longer had the power to hold him back.

With a deep breath, Noah pulled the door open and stepped inside.

ABOUT THE AUTHOR

Ben Hafer's books invite readers into immersive worlds filled with adventure and a deep exploration of human resilience. With a strong background in sci- ence and technology, each of his stories blends captivating  characters with intricate plots that challenge how we perceive reality and explore the depths of human consciousness. His writing is rooted in modern scientific details, appealing to readers who are passionate about advanced technology and the mysteries of the human experience. Ben often features complex virtual and alternate realities, examining how humanity and artificial intelligence intersect while exploring what it means to be alive in a rapidly evolving technological era.

BenHafer.com

www.ingramcontent.com/pod-product-compliance
Lightning Source LLC
Chambersburg PA
CBHW050329110726
47899CB00007B/2423